Standing in the Cold

Nasrin Mahoutchi-Hosaini

Standing in the Cold

Acknowledgements

Some of these stories have been previously published as follows:
Standing in the Cold: *The Best Australian Stories*, ed. Charlotte Wood,
Black Inc, Carlton, 2016
Kohl: *Overland*, Online, 237.5, Autumn Fiction, editorial by Allan Drew
01/04/2020. https://overland.org.au/previous-issues/issue-237-5-autumn-fic-
tion/2020
Fresh Food People: *Southerly*, Volume 77, Number 3, 2017
A Clear Darkness: in 'Persian Passages', *Southerly*, Volume 76,
3 November 2016
Satan Hill: in 'Getting it Right', *Heat*, Number 10, New Series, 2005
Delirium: *Heat*, Number 13, Series 2, 2007

Standing in the Cold
ISBN 978 1 76109 298 5

Cover photo by Nahid Moayerizadeh Ahmadi: Pigeon House, Yazo, Iran

First published 2022 by
GINNINDERRA PRESS
PO Box 3461 Port Adelaide 5015
www.ginninderrapress.com.au

Contents

Standing in the Cold

One Thursday, when Mr Razi had emerged from the subway to walk to his home, he saw that the snow had descended from the mountains and covered the streets. He tucked his head into his wool overcoat and his thick silver white hair ruffled out above his collar like a Shahin's open wings. He walked away from the main road and the sound of trains followed on the breath of the snow. He played with the corner of the metro ticket and then submerged his hands deep into his pockets and caressed his keys.

On the way home, he stopped at the corner shop to buy eggs and then he went to the local chemist to buy his new sleeping pills.

'I will give you the foreign brand, the imported one, the good one, not the generic one,' the chemist had promised.

Mr Razi watched those bony hands put the Zaleplon into a plastic bag. 'It is hypnotic. *Mesleh yek mordeh mekhabonatet, hichi nemifahmi.*'

Although Mr Razi had lived in the Meeremad area ever since he married Mrs Razi thirty-five years ago, he didn't have any friends in the neighbourhood. All the old neighbours moved out and the newcomers didn't show any interest in befriending an old man who wouldn't speak any more than a few words. Mr Razi felt he had nothing to talk about to his new neighbours. The only person Mr Razi knew in the area was Mrs Fars, an elderly woman who lived alone after all her family moved to America. Her eldest son demolished their home and made a five-storey building for his mother. Now Mrs Fars, who hardly could walk, sat on her first-floor kitchen and watched the neighbours.

*

When he turned into his street, he saw the shadow of his house under the dim streetlight. He lived in a two-storey house built with cheap red-yellowish bricks. This house plus the one on the right-hand side were the only old buildings left from the 60s. The rest of the old houses in the street were demolished and rebuilt as four- or five-storey apartment buildings.

He took out his key. Then he remembered that he had forgotten to pick up Mrs Fars's kidney medicine from the chemist. *I will find an excuse to explain it to her,* he thought.

He entered the *hayat*, which was covered in snow. His footsteps crunched. The plastic bag he was carrying brushed against the bare rose bushes. He flicked at a branch with his key and snow fell from the branch. Then he reached the veranda, he cleaned his feet on a *Khosh amedid* doormat, opened the door and entered the hallway. He locked the door behind him and dropped the key into his pocket.

The living room was furnished with a two-seat sofa and three armchairs with a light wood frame and a floral fabric. In the corner of a wall pictures of Van Gogh's *Sunflowers* and *Starry Night* were lost amongst numerous Gobelin tapestries which were covered all the walls. A large Gobelin of *The Last Supper* was framed in green-golden Baroque style. Mrs Razi finished the tapestries four years ago. Her first heart attack had prevented her from going back to the *Pardokht* girls' high, where she had taught year 12 ever since her marriage. She took art classes. The art classes were organised with their next-door neighbour's wife.

Mr Razi loved his wife's artworks. He didn't care that all the other neighbours' living rooms were decorated with the same objects made by the neighbourhood wives at the art classes.

The coffee tables were light-coloured wood; the china cabinet was a bit darker. On all the coffee tables stood a tissue box with handmade lace tissue covers, all in light green to match the light green curtains. In the two years before a series of heart attacks killed her, she spent all her time on her art and craft.

'You have to send me an email every night and tell me what you watched online,' the niece said. 'It is a new world, uncle. You should be part of it. You can follow the news online. I know you don't watch news on TV since your TV was broken. Believe me, you don't need TV, you can watch everything on the internet now.'

He purchased the laptop by selling some of his wife's jewellery. To show his appreciation for helping him to buy and learn how to use the internet, he gave his niece one of his wife's favourite rings. 'She loved you.' He watched the young hand wearing the golden ring. He kissed her face. 'You are like my own daughter.'

He kept his office the way Mrs Razi kept it. Above his working desk there were his Bachelor of Economics and diploma for chemical factory auditing framed in the same light green. Mrs Razi's diploma of teaching and certificate of tailoring were kept in the box of her sewing machine.

In the kitchen, he boiled two eggs and made a pot of jasmine tea, put it on a plastic tray and took it to his bedroom with the laptop. Sitting in bed, he watched the news on the internet. 'War, war, war, killing, killing everywhere. What a world is this?' He talked loudly as if talking to someone. Then he opened his email and sent an email to his niece.

'My dear Homma, I watched the news online, as you showed me to do it. News all over the world is horrible. Watching news online didn't leave any hope in me. I think I was happier when I didn't have TV to watch all the animosity human beings all around the world are facing these days. But sending an email to you every night is exciting. From your old uncle.'

Then he took two Zaleplon and hoped to sleep as the chemist promised him. He slept at the left side of the bed. The right side of the bed remained untouched.

He spent the next three days in bed. He only left his room once to make tea, pour it into his flask and bring it to his bedside table.

*

On the next day, snow continued and he didn't go out. In the kitchen, he made scrambled eggs and while eating he walked to his living room. His courtyard was framed in tall glass windows; it was quiet and the snow obscured the skyline and the land, white flakes falling from unseen origins. Then he watched the weather news on his laptop. The next days would be cloudy with possible snow. He sent an email to his niece.

'I can't come out in this weather. Tell your mum I won't come tonight. Love you both, goodbye.'

He turned off the laptop and in his mind he heard his niece's voice: *Dear uncle, take care of this computer and be careful not to spill water or tea. Just be careful, sometimes you can be like my mum, a bit forgetful.* He took another two sleeping pills from his bedside drawer and took them with his tea. Just before he turned the bedside light off, he heard the doorbell.

At first, he imagined he was hearing echoes, as he did when he didn't sleep deeply. Then he thought it must have been a mistake and whoever was behind the door would go away. But the bell rang again. He looked at his bedside silver clock. It was five past eleven. The bell kept ringing. He pulled his wool robe and wool slippers on and when he reached his hallway he pulled a brown wool throw from the corner of the sofa and covered himself with it. He walked through the *hayat*. The thorns of the rose bushes clutched at his robe.

His fingers frosted to the iron handle of the *hayat*'s gate. The bell rang again. He couldn't remember the last time he had had a visitor.

'Who is there?' he said, still holding the doorknob.

'Hello. Sorry to bother you this time, so late. It is late, isn't it?'

'Yes, it is. How can I help you?'

'Again, I am sorry to bother you this late. I am your next-door neighbour.'

He opened the door slowly. There was a young woman, standing on the other side of the gate. Her gloved fingers pointed to an old building pressed between apartment blocks on the other side of the street.

'I know you don't know me. I am Lili. My internet is disconnected. You know, I had to pay for my mother's medicine. So I thought if it is OK with you, I use your computer to talk to my sister. She lives in Australia. I have to ask her to send money.'

Ms Lili was pushing Mr Razi aside and was already in the *hayat*.

Mr Razi was trying to process this conversation and at the same time was trying to remain calm and courteous. But he had heard that recently some robbery had happened in the neighbourhood, so he had to be careful. He was holding the door firmly; he was wondering if she might push the door open.

'But, miss. Sorry, I am sorry, but I don't know you and it is very late. Can you call your sister tomorrow?'

Ms Lili was almost in the entrance to the hallway of the house. 'It is really cold here. Can we talk inside?'

Mr Razi's fingers, still cold, let the stranger enter his hallway. He locked the door and put the keys inside his nightgown pocket. In the hallway, he took his throw off his head and took his shoes off.

The young woman followed him to the living room. 'Ah, it's so warm and nice here.'

Mr Razi turned the living room's lights on. Ms Lili bit off her blue wool gloves and removed her headscarf, overcoat and boots.

'Here, you can leave them here,' said Mr Razi, taking Ms Lili's snow-covered boots and left them inside the shoe cabinet.

Ms Lili moved towards a sofa and sat there.

Mr Razi was moving awkwardly around. 'Do you need anything? I mean, can I offer you something?'

'Yes, please – a cup of tea, if you don't mind.'

Mr Razi did mind. It was almost midnight. But he was obliged to make the tea for this stranger.

While boiling the water, he looked through his kitchen window. The snow had stopped. He wiped the fog from the window. He realised that Mrs Fars's kitchen light was on. In fact, he saw that she was sitting there, watching him. *Has she seen this girl enter my house?*

When he entered the living room, Ms Lili was sitting on the sofa with her legs crossed and the throw on her legs. She had the Razi's wedding photo frame in her hand.

'Is this your daughter and her husband?' She stared at the photo.

'No, she is my wife.' He took the photo and put it on the table.

'She was my wife. She is dead. I don't have children. We don't have children.'

She stared at him. 'Is this you? No way!' The stranger girl almost shouted.

Her surprise annoyed Mr Razi.

Then the girl realised that might have been rude. 'I mean, you were so young when you married. And your wife, oh my god, she is pretty.'

She stopped and corrected herself. 'I mean, she was a beautiful woman.'

'Yes, my wife' he grunted, pushing the tea at her in exchange for the frame.

She noticed he was shaking. 'I am cold too. It seems that this winter never will come to the end.' Then she took the lid from a crystal bowl and scooped out two chocolates.

'I will bring my laptop and you can use the Skype for a moment only,' he said.

He went to his office, and when he returned the stranger was walking around the living room, checking the objects on the entertainment unit, the photos, DVDs. She pressed the CD player's play button; the 'Golden Dream' by Javad Ma'roofi played; she turned it off. Then she took the wedding photo frame again. Mr Razi didn't know how to ask her politely not to touch it.

'You two look very nervous in this photo. Were you nervous on your wedding day?'

'Here, the internet is connected. You can call your sister now.'

'Can I have another tea please?' And then she took her cup and walked towards the kitchen.

Mr Razi walked after her to take the cup from her, but she was already in the kitchen, pouring her tea and helping herself to biscuits, which he had placed on a china plate.

'This is nice.'

'Yes, yes. I buy them from the market at the Freedom square.'

'Oh, no, not the biscuits – they are nice too, but I was talking about your kitchen.'

She finished her tea. Then she sat on the chair, her back towards the heater.

'Please, Ms…? Sorry – what was your name again? It is very late. Maybe if you talk to your sister now – I, I have to go to bed.'

'Do you have to work in the morning?'

'No, I don't – I mean, I don't work outside any more. I do some consulting work from home.' He was annoyed at himself for answering her question.

'When did you retire?' She took another biscuit from the plate. 'My father retired at age fifty. He was sick. We don't know what went wrong with him, but the doctors said it was something in his heart. My mother never worked. She is sick and is in a wheelchair. One reason we came to this house is because there are no steps.'

Mr Razi was feeling very dizzy and sleepy. He couldn't ask her directly to leave; he had never asked anybody to leave his home before.

'Sorry, Ms Lili. It is lovely to listen to you but it is very late and I have to go to bed. Can you please use the internet and go? I am so sorry, I hope you don't think I am rude, but I really have to go to bed.'

'Oh, I am so sorry to bother you. Certainly, I will leave now. I will come back tomorrow to talk to my sister because I think she will be out now. The time difference between here and Australia is a headache. When it is night here, it is day there and my sister is at work. And when it is night there and day here, I can't leave my mother alone to come here to talk. I will come back tomorrow night.'

Then she put her wool overcoat, scarf and gloves, opened the shoe cabinet and pulled out her boots. 'Don't bother to let me out. I know the way out.'

The next day was Wednesday. When Mrs Razi was alive, she used to have a cleaner on Wednesdays. Mr Razi kept this tradition but he knew because of the snow the cleaner would not turn up. So, after drinking his morning tea, he decided to clean the house himself. He found the dusting sponge, the carpet cleaner and the blind cleaner inside a small plastic blue basket in the kitchen cabinet under the sink. There was a bag of white nylon gloves too, but he didn't bother with that.

First he dusted the wooden cabinet. After dusting the CD player, he played 'Golden Dreams'. At lunchtime, he scrambled eggs and ate them with cucumber pickles while watching the street through the kitchen window. He couldn't see Mrs Fars any more, but her kitchen light was still on. He wanted to check the news online but remembered some unbalanced mood that lingered around him last time when he watched the world news. He was feeling exhausted, so he decided to take his pills and go to bed.

He didn't know how long he had slept when the bell rang.

'Oh my god, it is her again.' He covered himself with wool and walked slowly through the snow into the *hayat*. The snow beneath his feet sounded as if someone was grinding something in their mouth.

'Who is it?'

'It's me, your next-door neighbour.'

'Sorry, miss, I am going to bed. As a matter of fact, I was in bed, asleep, and you woke me up. Can you please leave?'

'Please, sir, open the door. It is freezing here.'

'Yes, it is freezing here too. Please, I beg you, young lady, go home.'

'Please open the door. Something happened to my mum today.'

The softness of her voice made him go back and get his keys to open the door.

'What happened to your mother?'

Mr Razi was rugged up, and covered in snow. It made her heart break. She put her arm around him and softly pulled him with herself. On the way, she flicked at a branch with her finger and snow fell from the branch. Mr Razi rushed to open the hallway door; a bare branch clung to his wool shawl. He pulled the corner of the wool and freed himself.

Inside, she went to the kitchen, and Mr Razi followed her, still in shock from seeing this stranger in his home again. Lili made tea.

He watched Lili pull out the plastic step, which his wife used to reach the higher cabinet. When she stood on her toes, Mr Razi saw the soft roundness of her bare heels.

*

After five days of deep sleep, Mr Razi decided to go out. There was nothing left to eat. He needed more eggs, toilet paper, toothpaste and some cleaning items. He also needed more sleeping pills. He checked his medical insurance booklet and made sure it was in his pocket. In the kitchen, he checked the weather though the window. The sky had emerged, seemingly deeper, and darker, than before the coming of the mountain snows. Sparrows darted between the electricity lines, which had emerged from beneath a membrane of snow. He grinded some dried bread in the palm of his hands and tossed it into the *hayat*. Still, the street was empty except for the bustle of the snow cleaners.

After he finished his morning tea, he took the shopping list and his medical insurance booklet and put them in his wool overcoat. He wrapped his neck with his shawl and took his key and left his hallway. The snow still dusted the footpath through the forecourt. He pushed some snow from a rose branch with his glove-covered finger and left his home. *She is very strange, this new neighbour. Maybe it isn't such a bad idea if I just knock on the door and introduce myself to her mother. Poor crippled woman. I hope I never get put in a wheelchair. Awful.*

He walked only two or three steps, and stopped with a shock.

The neighbour's house had been demolished and was covered with snow. Corners of broken bricks and tiles and a broken pieces of bathroom were strewn across the lot.

He walked towards the rubble and called, 'Ms Lili! Ms Lili, where are you?'

An old peddler woman was walking past, selling handkerchiefs. She came closer to Mr Razi.

He pulled out a few coins to offer her.

'Do you want to buy?'

'No thanks.'

'Then I hope God makes your house worse than this.'

He knocked on Mrs Fars's door. No answer. Then he walked towards the chemist shop.

'There you are. I just knocked on your door looking for you,' he said when he walked inside the chemist. Mrs Fars was sitting on a metal chair waiting for her prescription to be prepared. She was covered with her heavy wools. Her small wrinkly face looked like an old turtle's face covered in a wool shell.

'Mrs Fars, I am so sorry about not picking up your medicine last time.'

'Which medicine? When?'

'Mrs Fars, what has happened to our neighbour?'

'Which neighbour? The young couple upstairs? Oh, they are fighting again over their divorce. So you could hear them too? I told the police. You know, I was the one who called the police. They came late of course. So if you have heard them from the other side of the street, no doubt my other upstairs neighbour should have heard them too, but when the police questioned her, she said she had heard nothing.'

Mrs Fars's prescription was ready. She walked toward the cashier but she was too short to reach the desk. Mr Razi took the money and her medical insurance booklet and handed it to the girl behind the cashier desk. Then he helped her out, holding her arm.

'Mrs Fars, I am not talking about your neighbour in your building. I am asking about Ms Lili's family, my next-door neighbour.'

Mrs Fars's arm in Mr Razi's hand felt light as a twig. The distance from the chemist to their homes was only a few streets but even that was too long for Mrs Fars, especially with this snow.

'Can we catch a taxi?' she asked, like a little girl asking for a doll.

Mr Razi stopped at the corner of the street to check for a taxi.

'There is no taxi. I don't think in this weather anyone comes out of their home. We better walk, otherwise we will freeze. Why did you come in this weather?' he asked.

'I didn't realise that I didn't have any painkiller. My rheumatism is unbearable. At my age, my children should be around me to help me. But as you know, these days, whoever can run away from this place, they will do it at any cost.' Then she pressed Mr Razi's arm even firmer, to stop herself from falling into the piled-up snow.

'Yes, I know, Mrs Fars, how you feel. I don't have children.'

Then his face moved towards Mrs Fars for confirmation. 'Since my wife passed away, I feel so lonely in this world. I can't sleep at nights. That is why I came out in this weather, to buy more sleeping pills.'

They turned onto their street.

'Mrs Fars, where are Ms Lili's family? Where did they go? When did they demolish the building?'

Mrs Fars stopped. 'Mr Razi, what is the matter with you? The house next door to yours has been empty for the last five years. Don't you re-member? Don't you recall the day? It was your wife's funeral. The car stopped in front of the building, and the last resident asked you to move the car because of the removalist van? Don't you remember?'

Mr Razi's eyes moved over Mrs Fars as if he could not recognise her.

'Mr Razi, are you all right? Let's get inside. Come in and have a tea?'

'Oh, no, I don't want to trouble you. But please, answer me again – you didn't tell me what happened to Ms Lili and her family.'

He was holding Mrs Fars's thin arm to help her to walk the few steps in her front door.

'Mr Razi who is Ms Lili? Who are you talking about?'

'The next-door neighbour. I am talking about the next-door neigh-bour. My next-door neighbour. The girl. There is this young lady, her name is Ms Lili, and in the last few nights she came to visit me.'

Mrs Fars pulled out her arm from Mr Razi's hand. Then she looked at his eyes with astonishment and blame. 'Mr Razi, aren't you ashamed of yourself? You are a respectable man. We knew each other for years. Your wife, your beautiful wife, was such a respectful woman too.'

Mr Razi was annoyed that this old neighbour was questioning his loyalty to his wife, but he didn't have time or patience to discuss that now. He wanted to know what had happened to Ms Lili.

'Mrs Fars, I didn't mean that kind of visit. She came to use my in-ternet because she didn't have an internet connection and she wanted to talk to her sister in Australia.'

'Mr Razi, I am telling you, there was no neighbour in the house next door to yours for months and months. There is no Ms Lili there, for sure, I am telling you. If there was any neighbour, I would be the first one to know.' Then she went in.

Mr Razi walked towards the demolished house and stared at the broken tiles and bricks. He stood there until the cold penetrated his woollen coat. He left the debris and went home.

In the kitchen, he boiled the water and made tea. He took two sleeping pills from his coat pocket and had them with his tea.

When he had just fallen asleep, the bell rang. He thought his ears wrong. He ignored it. But the bell rang and rang. He finally got out of his bed, covered himself in the wool blanket and went out to open the door. He heard the door lock behind him. He fiddled with the door-knob, pressed it, pushed it, but the door was locked. Mr Razi stood in the freezing air, but he no longer felt cold.

Kohl

I have a hearing problem. I can hear the smallest movement of water as if it were the sound of an ocean. I've often wondered if it was because I was born nearly three weeks late. I was delivered by a midwife on the cusp of the forty-third week of mother's pregnancy.

A new package arrived by post yesterday morning. It was a cardboard box covered with clear masking tape. I opened the box with a knife and carefully pulled out a Kats extractor for removing foreign bodies from nasal cavities. We already had one in the surgery but it was old and we needed a new one. I had also ordered a pair of Asch's septum forceps which my husband Omid, an otolaryngologist, uses to work on his patients with deviated nasal septum. In a separate package there was an aural syringe, an instrument for preventing blood flow by compressing the blood vessels, as well as three head mirrors with headbands and two forceps.

After inspecting each item, I carefully put the products back in the box. They were expensive, especially with our currency. There was also a catalogue. It was in the English language. It was part of my job to translate the catalogue into Farsi for Omid so he could keep up to date, but I put it to one side. It was lunchtime, and I was hungry.

When we were first married, Omid discovered he didn't care much for my home-cooked meals, so we ate out. We ate in local eating houses called *Jigaraki*. They had only a choice of one or two items, either sheep kidneys or livers roasted over charcoal. The smell of it was as if your own kidneys and liver were on fire. We would sit inside at one of the small tables which each had a small vase with plastic bouquets of red and pink carnations.

We married just after my husband finished medical school and qualified as an ENT specialist. I became his assistant and secretary as well as his wife.

At that time, his surgery – I mean our surgery – was a small room in front of our old small house in central Tehran. My reception desk was in the very corner of the room, right beside the four chairs for waiting patients. Behind a wooden partition that divided the room in half were his desk and the examination bed. Behind the surgery was our living room, divided into a dining room, and our bedroom, divided by another wooden partition, was at the back of the house. With my own money, I bought a dressing table with a mirror at a second-hand shop and put it in the bedroom.

After Omid had risen for his morning walk, I could stay in bed till an extra hour before the patients arrived. Before going to the surgery, I always looked at myself to make sure my hair was pinned back, my foundation light and my eyes kohled.

'Presentation is important, especially for a woman, for a doctor's assistant,' that was how Omid put it.

He always wore three-piece suits and shaved with a cut-throat. He looked in the mirror more than I did, fixing his tie, combing his hair with the palm of his hand and adjusting his rimless glasses.

'I think it would be good to have two mirrors, one for you and one for me,' I once suggested.

'What?'

'Because we both have to get ready at the same time and you need the mirror as much as me, I think it would be good to have two dressing mirrors,' I said.

He walked out without responding.

He was a new doctor and we were new in the area. Most of our patients were men, mainly old men, but sometimes patients who, though young, were going deaf. Almost all the old patients used to wear thick-rimmed glasses. Those who needed nasal examinations had to take off their glasses to make it easier for my husband to examine them. I usually stood at the top of the chair, behind them, holding the tray of various forceps. I used to watch patients close their eyes when the corner of the metal levers reached them to press their nostrils open. At the top of their noses they all had a rim print, an arc, like a skin bridge between two eyes. Sometimes I imagined one eye walking out of its socket, crossing the bridge of the nose and overlapping the other eye. As if the top eye was watching the bottom eye but the bottom eye couldn't watch because it was closed by the top eye.

Hearing aids were new to the market and my husband was good at implanting them. Beside his work as a specialist, he also imported medical devices, such as stethoscopes, pen torches and forceps to then distribute to other doctors at a slight profit. In those days, as a result of working with people with hearing problems, my tone of voice had risen three times higher. I was constantly shouting at the patients, as they held the palm of their hand curved to capture the air which carried the sound. Have you seen the shape of the palm that people with hearing problems make? They bend the palm of their hand as if it were a trumpet. Actually, the first hearing aid was called a trumpet.

My husband had a poster of different hearing aids on the wall. He brought it with him when he came back from medical school in India. Many people who couldn't afford to go to medical schools in Europe would go to either India or Turkey to complete their education. In Mumbai, he treated dozens of people with hearing loss every day, but mostly he syringed wax.

My hearing problem wasn't fixable with a hearing aid.

'It is more in your head than in your ear,' my husband told me.

One day when the business was doing better, when Omid and I were sitting in the park after eating our charcoal chicken livers and kidneys, he said that after he returned from his medical conference in Turkey, we would go on a cruise from Istanbul to Europe. 'It is a good way to deal with your problem. Trust me. It will help to stop the water slapping in your head.'

I just looked at him.

Once, he wanted to clean a patient's ears to remove excessive wax. He said, 'Dear, please prepare the tray. We have to irrigate Mr L's ears.'

I had read and read about the procedure and I was confident I could help. But as soon as my husband started to use a stream of warm water, I fainted. I could hear an entire ocean storm inside, something that had started as no more than a whisper in childhood, like when you put a conch to your ear, but that since my marriage to Omid had reached gargantuan proportions. After that event, I couldn't eat properly for a few days. Anytime I wanted to chew my food, I would hear the storm again. I never heard the ocean with those patients who needed their noses examined. For example, I never heard the sound of a storm when my husband was cauterising nasal cavities or removing polyps.

Little by little, we increased our patients. Now, women came too as well as their children. I wanted to assist Omid, but that storm wave re-emerged any time I saw my husband getting close to someone's ear or throat.

Once, when examining eighty-five-year-old Mr M, Omid asked me to hold the pen torch for him. We knew Mr M very well. His shop was in the middle of an arcade in the bazaar. Anytime I walked passed his shop to go to my parents' home on the other side of the bazaar, I passed through the steady banging of artisans engaging in *Galamzani*. They supplied the embossed copper plates and trays to the local restaurants and *Jigaraki* in the area. Mr M was the master. Before he sat on the ex-amination table, he gave me a copper tray embossed with grapes and dates. I pressed my hand against Mr M's hand. I knew he didn't have money to pay for his visit. *Galamzani* was dying in the area as most restaurants had started using china and the *Jigaraki* used plastic and melamine plates. I put the plate on the table, and then helped Mr M ready for his examination.

Mr M complained about a wheezy noise in his ears.

'Now, Mr M, I can see that the canal in the middle ear is infected. The transfer of *seda* waves has been affected and that's the reason you feel a sound in your head.'

My husband reached for the medium-sized forceps, a torch, some cotton and a bottle of alcohol and asked Mr M to keep his mouth open wide. He asked me to keep the torch closer to the patient's mouth.

Omid also had a torch on above his head on his medical hat. 'You know, what I see is that the tympanic membrane has been affected too.'

While Omid was talking, I could see inside Mr M's throat, the lines on his upper and lower parts of his mouth, arcs of flesh. I could see a dam was breaking inside his mouth and felt the rising torrent of a tidal wave above me. I lost the torch.

When I woke up, it was evening. I was in my bed and my husband was sitting beside me.

'What happened? Did you have the water sound issue again?'

'I am sorry, dear.'

'No, I am sorry. I shouldn't have asked you to help me with Mr M.'

He brought me some rice with potato and charcoaled kidney and liver. I hadn't eaten for a few days. But when I brought the flesh to my mouth, the sound of water in my ear came back.

'I am not hungry.'

'But you should eat something. You can't go on like this.'

I watched his fingers combine the liver and potatoes. He tried to hand-feed me. 'We need to have someone to help us. Poor Mr M thought you fainted because he squeezed your hand too hard.'

'But I am OK. I will help you.'

He left the room without answering me.

*

One day, a big box was delivered by post, much bigger than our usual packages. It was a glass aquarium. Inside the box there was an air pump and electrical wires. There was a catalogue describing codes of the glass type, electricity specification for artificial lights, and descriptions about aeration, filtration and how to heat the water.

Omid went out at lunchtime that day and brought home two tropical fish in a plastic bag. I was looking at him while he was setting it up – the glass box, the plastic trees, and the sand. I watched as he plugged in the electricity, the bubbles coming out of the pump, the red and green lights turning on. Then he filled it with water. I tried not to close my ears. I tried not to let the sound of water scare me.

When the water was warm enough, he took two tropical fish from the water in a plastic bag and dropped them in the aquarium. The two fish danced against each other and hid behind the plastic trees. We both watched them for a while.

'Do you like it? I set the aquarium on your dressing table, close to our bed.'

'Why?'

'Because when the room is quiet, you will hear the water and its movements and gradually you will get used to it and, because you are safe, lying down in the bed next to me, you will see that the sound of water can be peaceful.'

I tried to focus on the fish, watching the two little creatures move around, kiss the wall of the glass with their little red lips and run away and hide behind the plastic tree.

My husband checked his face in the mirror and combed his hair upward with the palm of his hand and adjusted his glasses on the arc of his nose. He touched his shaved jaw and went out.

For the first few weeks, I didn't sleep. The sound of the water inside the aquarium was running inside me, not only into my ears but also into my body. As soon as I closed my eyes, I had a feeling as if I was drowning. I shifted closer to my husband, feeling that if one side of my body was blocked from the water, I would be safe.

Months passed and gradually I learnt to sleep with the aquarium in our bedroom. I think I was improving. Still I couldn't assist my husband in the surgery. We both decided that it was better that I focus on the purchasing and distributing of the equipment and the translating of the medical brochures.

One day, an old woman came in. She had dishevelled hair and stank. She wore a long green floral skirt, a red wool top, and a coloured patterned jacket. She looked like a charity box. She couldn't speak Farsi and from just the two words she said, 'Doctor, pain,' I knew that she was Azari. So I spoke with her in the Azari language. My husband started asking questions and I translated. She was perspiring so badly it was as if there was a shower on in her body. She also said she was very thirsty. I brought her water, which she drank in one go. I heard the water in her throat. After many questions and translations, it turned out that she was in the wrong surgery. She had chest and heart pain. My husband had to refer her to another local doctor.

After she left, I started to hear the water again and the image of her drinking water and the sound of it possessed me.

*

He hired a new assistant. A young girl from our neighbourhood.

I spent hours on product catalogues: hearing aids, torches and forceps. I was in contact with many doctors and suppliers. I heard the storm less and less.

One day, my husband and his young assistant were busy in the examination room and I was busy in my own little corner with my catalogues. I had finished my translation and a sample of a new glossy catalogue had arrived from the printer. It looked good but they had missed some of the photos I had asked them to include. For example, they forgot to print the photo of the old stethoscope. The old one was amazing; it was like a large drain plunger I use in the kitchen. I thought that photo should be printed next to the new one.

We didn't have time to close the surgery for lunch any more. More businesses were coming to the area and the area became very crowded and everybody had to wait a long time in the queue for *Jigaraki* or restaurants to eat lunch. As a result of missing lunch more frequently, I was losing weight and my husband was losing his temper more often.

One day, the young assistant came with a piece of paper in her hand. 'Look, we have takeaway in the area now.'

We stared at her.

'It's very common overseas. Last year, I went to America with my parents and I found out how good this takeaway is. They also have home delivery.'

She showed us a brochure, like our medical brochures, I thought.

'This is a takeaway menu.'

Menu back then was a new word for me. It was a list of different foods categorised into different sections: meat with rice, pasta with different sauces, seafood.

The young assistant was looking at us as if she had discovered a possible cure for a disease. 'How about *gazaye-daryaei*?'

My husband and I looked at each other and decided to leave it to her to do the order.

After a few short sentences exchanged with someone on the phone, she said, 'It is done.'

Fifteen minutes later, our food arrived.

While she put the napkins, plastic cutlery and soft drinks on the table, she said, 'This is snapper, very delicious, it is like our *Mahi sefid* from the north. I'm from the north and I like fish from the north of the Caspian Sea, but god, it's very expensive these days.'

I was staring at the fish, its head and eyes burned by the charcoal flame.

She took the whole body of the fish and laid it on a big tray. First she made a hole on the upper layer of the skin and then sliced through the middle of the body and removed the line of bones. We started eating. The young assistant moved her long fingers into the body of the fish, excavating the flesh. Omid took off the burned skin off from the middle of the fish and ate some of it with his hand. I squashed the flesh between my fingers before putting it in my mouth, but on my second mouthful I felt a bone lodge in my throat. I wanted to cough it out but I couldn't. My breathing was blocked but my eyes were clear and they followed my husband and his new assistant as they rushed to get the forceps.

'Wider, wider, darling,' my husband exhorted.

I did open my mouth, to the point of feeling that my jaw was dividing. I knew what the next step was, I have seen how professionally and delicately he used his equipment.

I felt the taste of cold metal in my throat. I could see within my mind's eye the two hands of the metal open and reach for the foreign bone stuck in the arc of my mouth. I felt my husband's forceps secure the bone, then heard him exhale. The new assistant looked at him with admiration. He dropped the bone into a silver tray and then he guided me towards our bedroom. My husband and I napped. When I finally woke up, my husband was gone.

I walked to the front surgery and saw the young assistant. She sat where I used to sit when I was an assistant. She was posting items and our correspondence. When I walked in, she didn't raise her head. I looked at her and then I realised – I couldn't remember her from when my husband and I interviewed for the position.

'I can't remember you.'

'Sorry, what did you say?' Her eyes were still on papers and letters.

I watched her finger the letter opener. 'I mean, I can't remember seeing you in the interview process. I remember those young girls came in for interview but you were not one of them. Am I right?'

'Yes, you are right.' She put down the letter opener and rose up, fixing her white coat's hem which had rolled up her thighs as she sat. She then walked over and stood in front of the mirror, fixing the corner of her short black hair with her long fingers.

'Why weren't you there? How did you get the job?'

'Mr Doctor employed me.' She opened the medicine cabinet. The smell of alcohol and metal came into the air.

'My husband employed you without me being here?'

She put an alcohol bottle and some cotton balls into a tray. 'Yes. The day I came here you were not here.' Then she stooped, walked around and faced me. 'Mr Doctor told my father he needed an assistant. My father was his patient and he told Mr Doctor about me.' As she was speaking, she moved to the area behind the partition. She put some flakes into the aquarium.

I watched the tropical fish come out of their hidden area behind the plastic tree, nibbling the food with their red lips.

'When I came, Mr Doctor didn't interview me. He just started to explain my duties.' She sat down at my desk again and took out a patient's files.

I looked at her. She lowered her eyes.

A little later that day, I decided to go for a walk. I crossed the surgery room. Behind the screen, my husband was working on a patient's throat. The assistant was standing behind the patient with a tray of forceps and a torch in her hand. I didn't say anything.

I walked through the bazaar to my father's home. In the late afternoon, some shopkeepers were closing up. The *gegaraki* was arranging his chicken kidneys on a tray. His young assistant lit new charcoals; a few sparks flew went into the air. I stopped at another shop and bought some nuts for my father. I pointed and the shopkeeper took a pile of hazelnuts, pistachios and almonds and poured them inside the paper bag. I watched his wrinkled hand submerge deep into the hessian bag and emerge holding the mixed nuts, like hands that offer food on holy days. I walked past the shop where my mother used to send me to have the kitchen knives and scissors sharpened. The shopkeeper shook his head towards me to say hello.

I stayed for a while with my father, drinking black tea with cube sugars, eating the nuts from a tray. I walked back through the bazaar and came back home in the evening.

I entered our living room. Early evening light was coming through the window. I called my husband's name quietly. No answer. I took my jacket off and looked at the pile of mail. It was strange that there wasn't the usual sound of the aquarium. It was the time to feed the fish. For a while, I watched the two tropical fish swim around the plastic tree, I took a glass of water from the fridge and drank it. My hunger had returned and I felt like eating out with my husband, just the two of us, alone.

I went to the surgery and I started cleaning up, putting the equipment into the alcohol to be washed for tomorrow. I put the plug in the sink and turned on the tap. One by one, I put some plates and glasses inside the sink to wash them, but slipped the Kats forceps into the pocket of my lab coat, instead of dropping them into the alcohol.

On the table, there was some lunch left over and the bone my husband took out of my throat was still sitting in a tray. I wrapped all of it up into the takeaway paper and threw in the package into the bin. All of a sudden, I heard the sound of water. I returned to the sink, which was overflowing, the water running over the sink and onto the floor. I turned off the tap.

Then I remembered I hadn't yet fed the fish, so I returned to our room and took out a pinch of the flakes from the brown bag. Standing over the aquarium, I let the flakes fall from my hand, far too many for two small fish. For a while, I watched the bubbles the fish made in the water, watched them feasting on the food floating on the surface, getting heavy and sinking. Deep in my lab coat pocket, the forceps were heavy against my thigh. I reached down into my pocket, my fingers feeling for the forceps, pulling them out. Without looking at the instrument, I felt thin metal handles between my fingers, I found myself opening and closing the forceps so their tips clanged surely but gently, raising the forceps to the height of the fish tank, poising the tips so they kissed the surface of the water. The thin coldness of the metal on my skin. The fish with their red lips gorging themselves on the food. The forceps in my fingers with a will of their own.

Fresh Food People

I don't drive any more. When my husband stops at Bigge Street in front of 2GLF Liverpool Radio, I massage my fingers with Voltaren gel. The smell lingers in the air-conditioned air of the car. When he returns to the car, the hot air comes in first. He drops a yellow folder on my lap; 2GLF has been printed on it in thick black ink. I recognise his handwriting. I turn over a page: 'The Migrant Stories of Regional Australia'. He has typed it in bold print.

On the six a.m. drive, the Cumberland Highway from Liverpool to the warehouse in Fairfield is filled with traffic. Traffic outside and talkback radio inside, which only shift workers and insomniacs listen to: topic of the day is lonely people and dogs.

We both yawn constantly.

He looks at me and smells the arthritis gel on my hands. 'Why don't you leave this job?'

'I will. When we buy our restaurant, then I will leave this bloody job.' I rub my hand with Voltaren gel again.

'Did you get your money back?'

'Not yet. We are trying. We will. We will. I know. Can we talk about it later? I really am not in the mood for this talk. Please don't start this again.'

'You started.'

'No, you did.'

'Okay then, I will finish it too.'

*

Piles of vegetables in boxes await the early morning knives; the ritual wash and slaughter for public consumption; delivery to private caterers; wedding venues, birthday parties and private houses. In this long warehouse, we cut, slice or shred carrots, cabbages, lettuce, eggplants, capsicums, cucumbers and zucchinis for our daily orders. From time to time, we get special orders for vegetables for barbecues or special requests from restaurants for the specific cutting of eggplants or zucchinis, but the main orders usually are just for salad mixes. The warehouse is divided into four sections: the unpacking of boxes and washing area, the cutting area, the packaging area, and the last one is our tea room. Our lockers and work gear are in this area. Big Jimmy, Jenny and I share this room.

The business belongs to Barry's brother. We never see him; Barry himself works with us. Instead of wearing the uniform work clothes – hats, gloves and apron – he always wears his usual clothes: Hawaiian shirt and baby-blue shorts he bought from Vinnie's. He always wears brown socks with his brown sandals, pulled to his knees. The pallor of his pinkish white skin is stamped with years of sun damage.

Barry doesn't eat with us. In fact, he comes to the tea room only to give us our pay cheques. We don't know why our boss has given his brother this responsibility but for sure Barry enjoys it. Every fortnight, on Friday evening he enters the tea room and when we open our envelopes, our money smells of petroleum. He doesn't like us – not that we did anything to cause that. It is just the way it is. He has a deep thick carpet of anger spread in his heart. He simply doesn't like anybody. Once, he picked a fight with a truck driver, a big guy, almost Barry's size. Thank god the truck driver ignored Barry's anger and left him with a few words.

'Maybe he was left under the sun too long when he was a little boy.' That is Big Jimmy's logic for Barry's everlasting anger.

Barry eats in the back of his truck. Every morning, he takes a can of dog food – beef, Coles brand, from his brown Coleman Cooler and leaves it in front of his dog, Massy, a brown German shepherd. He then opens a two-litre packet of Woolworths home brand milk and, while gulping it, he stares at his dog. He listens to Alan Jones's breakfast show on 2GB. For lunch, he repeats the same thing.

When I go to the tea room, Jimmy is there; his long black hair covered in a cheese net hat, his black apron hanging from his waist, his long hairy hands in plastic gloves. The 2GLF radio station is airing Indonesian-language news. He pretends to listen to the radio but his eyes are on the washing room. Big Jimmy has a special feeling for Jenny, like a small shiny marble that seems to shine in the corners of his black eyes whenever he looks at her; sometimes, I see the marble roll and drop into his mouth and he says, 'Jenny, you are doing very good job!' Or 'That dress suits you.' Sometimes, the marble rolls and falls into his stomach when he is in the packaging room and under the zip zip sound of plastic bags he sings Indonesian love songs, and sometimes it is under his long fingers when he plays with small soft tissues of cabbage while he looks at her. Both Barry and Big Jimmy glow whenever she is around. Big Jimmy is the main forklift driver but he also does produce purchasing from Flemington Market.

I put my handbag in the locker and cover myself with a big plastic apron. I see a pile of fish resting in the ice bath; almost fall on them.

'What is this? What are these doing here?' I look at the fish heads, sharp teeth, threatening even in their death.

'They are mine. On the way to work I went to the fish market.'

'Put the lid on it, please. They are looking at me.' I cover my hair in the net.

'They are fighting again.'

'When did this start?' I smell the plastic gloves on my fingers.

'I don't know. When I came, he was already here.'

I pretend that I don't care about another Barry-and-Jenny fight and start my work. The sound of an electric knife slices open my sleepy eyes. I reach the washing basins, turn on the tap and push carrots into one basin and cabbages into the other. The carrots stick to the corner of the sink; I push them; long condemned vegetables scramble on each other's heads and move into the silver basin. I pour the liquid soap; the smell of fake lemon juice presses into their orange skins. I go to the cabbages;

the vegetables are heavy and firm; I push them under the water. As soon as the sound of the electric knife stops, I hear Jenny crying. I run to her in the packaging room. Barry White has cornered her, his big red face at the level of her breast. His right hand holds her left wrist. He pushes her and Jenny falls down on a pile of Nutella chocolate cake boxes.

'Give me my money.'

'Barry, I swear.'

Now Barry straightens to his full height. There is thick anger in his fist. 'Give me my money or I will cut your useless Chinese face.'

Jenny is Vietnamese. Her Iranian husband spends most of his time at Liverpool and Fairfield RSL clubs and anytime he can get his hands on big money he is at Star City. Jenny borrowed money from Barry to pay part of her share of the deposit on a restaurant in Fairfield. Jenny's husband gambled and lost it. Her husband has disappeared and now Jenny works here and some other jobs to pay back Barry's money. But paying $5,000 back with rent and food and other bills to pay is not easy. Barry knew that; he knew Jenny's husband was a gambler and didn't care what would happen to her. He knew that Jenny would fall into his hands.

He moves away from her; kicks at the Nutella cake boxes; turns back and his eyes plunder the light.

Jenny collects her body from the floor. 'I am trying to find him. I have called his family.'

'Tomorrow. I want my money tomorrow.' He walks towards the door; his brown sandals make a slimy noise on the wet floor. The bundle of keys is dangling from his pocket. When he leaves, a wet anger leaves the room too.

I rush to the taps; the basins are overflowing. I turn the taps off. The next shift of people are standing at the door and watching us.

Jenny runs towards the bathroom, holding her mouth, 'This *Vo*, oh this *Vo*.'

In the workers' kitchen, we pick up shredded vegetables to take home.

Jenny collects her small body and walks like a broken mermaid into the washing room.

*

I drop a plastic bag of shredded vegetables on the table. I check my mail and email and voice mail. No news from our son.

In the shadow of the smell of the burning meat, I see my husband half naked in front of the barbecue. His chest hair is grey now and he is sweaty. Under the fray of the sun, the droplets on his chest looks like mercury beads. I think to myself, how quickly he got old. I remember those chest hairs once were black and shiny like a falcon's breast after flight.

He goes and brings a bundle of envelopes, leaves them on the outside table and goes back to his barbecue.

'Can I help?'

'Make salad.'

I knew he would give me that job, the easy one, something my stiffened fingers can manage. I empty the shredded vegetables into a bowl; I lift the brown Pyrex lid but my fingers freeze and pause. My hand looks like a perching bird and the pain percolates into the joints. I lose the lid. It shatters into pieces.

I want to clean the floor but can't. He does it and then makes the dressing. A cloggy smell of thick honey, crushed garlic and balsamic welds to the air.

'*In bohayeh khoob ham azeyatam mikone. Har booei dardam ro bishtar mikoneh.*' He looks at my fingers.

Jenny constantly says *Vo*. Even the good smell of food makes my pain grow. This *Vo*!

I hug him and the smell of his sweat reaches me.

'How can you cook in this weather?'

He knows I feel guilty. I haven't cooked since my arthritis started deforming my hands. I like cooking. It calms me down. But I can't.

In our bedroom, I see a dozen roses and a box of chocolates. It makes me angry.

I open the window; the smell of barbecue dances into my words.

'Don't do this. You know it makes me angry.'

'I know. Sorry I didn't have time to think of something else.'

'You know I hate that Woolworth's love story – Valentine's Day.' I look at the box with a heart on it. I drop it on the bed.

'A man without imagination should be shut away.' I can hear his laughter.

'Agreed.'

After a minute, he yells with heart-shaped laughter. 'Come and eat.'

It is late evening and the sun is still there. No sign of the night's birth. Heat and dry air stimulate dogs to bark in neighbours' backyards. He waters the backyard and wakes up mosquitoes. We go inside. He checks his emails and I know in his mind he is creating a lie.'

'He might have sent us an email but we didn't get it.

'No. It is not possible.'

I go to our son's room. There is a photo of him, taken by me. Before getting all these crooked fingers, I used to take lots of family photos. This one is my favourite. It is his twenty-first birthday. He looks like his father, only taller, with more restless eyes, but has the same dark hair, like his father when I met him; like a black eagle always thinking about flying far and high. After his first year at university, he decided to defer for one year and travel the world. Now, he is in South America, perhaps in Colombia – maybe – according to the basic timetable he gave us before leaving Sydney. But no news, no emails or phone calls. I enter his room, I pass the red Che Guevara and the black Bob Marley and through piles of university notebooks I find a piece of paper with some telephone numbers and hotel names on it. Before I leave the room, I notice a sticker with some hotel names and telephone numbers on it on the Australian soccer team poster. I take that too.

*

Big Jimmy's father came from Indonesia and when he committed suicide, Jimmy started working. He has been working since he was ten years old. The three of us had a plan. We decided to leave this job and start our own restaurant. It would work. Jenny is a fantastic cook; we all talk about the delicious food she made for us at last year's Christmas party. Big Jimmy is good with purchasing produce and I could manage the business. With my arthritis, I can't do this job any more. We saved money and gave it to Jenny. Jenny wanted more of a share and she borrowed from Barry. It was Jenny's husband who put the idea of the restaurant in our heads. He knew many restaurant owners in the Liverpool and Fairfield area. At that time, we didn't know Jenny's husband had a passion for gambling. Jenny wanted to open a business on her own but she couldn't afford it. Then she approached us. We gave her money for a deposit but her husband stole the money and lost it all in Star City.

Our plan was to buy the Ambassador Lounge in Fairfield, because it had a good business record.

'It is fantastic. Do you know how many weddings, engagements, birthdays and naming days they do there every year?' Jenny had been invited to weddings there before and she thinks the three of us could do good business.

*

We sit in the Angel café. The Neeta City shopping centre. It is hot again.

On our third Turkish coffee, finally Abdollah tells us the truth. 'Guys, he is not selling.' And then he takes out a piece of paper and drops it on the table. The smashed cigarette butts and café stains diffuse their smell and colour into the white paper.

'What is this?'

'This, my dear lady, is a new preposition for new business.'

'New proposition, you mean.'

'Ye, whatever. My English, hey. I am not professor but I am business man and good one, ye? Ye, Jenny? Ask Jenny, she knows I am a good business man.'

Jenny's tiny body wraps itself inside her shyness. I look at her face with surprise. I didn't know Jenny knew this guy that well. 'So you are bringing us a new business proposition. What is it?'

'Hey, Ali, bring coffee.' With the back of his hand, he cleans his side of the table, lights a cigarette, inhales and locks the smoke in his mouth behind his teeth. He smiles and looks at us.

Jenny turns her face the other way, pretending to look at the shops, away from the smoke which she has told me makes her feel nauseous. Big Jimmy is listening with attention and I am losing my patience.

'I don't want coffee.' I clean the mess in front of my table and push it towards Abdollah. 'Talk. What is it?'

'This coffee shop.'

I look around.

He brings his head very close to me and whispers, 'I have talked with the owner and he is prepared to give you guys a very good discount. He is in financial trouble and his wife wants to go back to Iraq, so he has to sell.'

The amount that sounds so reduced to him is in fact even higher than the price we were prepared to pay for the restaurant. I push the table away from me, towards him. My hands stiffen and I can't pick up my handbag; I walk, shouting to Big Jimmy to drive us away.

We are driving on the Cumberland Highway; traffic from Fairfield to Liverpool is running fast with big trucks. Then Big Jimmy's mobile rings.

'Hey, Jimmy, I want to talk to you but don't bring the grandmother with you.'

The phone is on speaker.

'Fuck you, Abdollah, we are coming to get our money back,' I scream.

Jimmy is shocked; I never swear, not even at work.

'Turn, turn, Jimmy. We are going to catch him.'

At the next lights, we turn. When we get to Neeta City, Abdollah is gone. I spot Jenny at the Afghani bakery with a big pile of flat breads; she is walking to her car.

'Jesus, you scared me,' she shouts when I sit beside her.

My dry, deformed fingers land on her soft skin and strong long shapely bones; the spider of my fingers webs her hand. She doesn't move.

'Look at me, Jenny. Look at me – whose baby is this?'

'Why you ask? You are not my mother.'

'No, but we are going to be business partners. I need to know.' My eyes have arrested her small courage. 'It's him, isn't it? It's Abdollah's baby.'

'He is good guy, honest guy. Why don't you trust him?'

'Trust him! You surprise me, Jenny. How much do you know him? Who introduced him to you?'

'It was your husband, wasn't it?'

My fingers spider over her hand onto her knee, and her fingers start to shake.

'He is honest man.'

'Like your husband. Like that bastard who took our money, your money too and ran away.'

*

Even at five a.m., the heat is strong. Everyone is doing two or three shifts. I walk to the main gate. The big lights are still on. I pass a group of men and women who are smoking in silence; too early for chat, but not for smoking – it's always a good time to smoke. I guide Big Jimmy to lift big boxes of plastic bags and boxes, zigzagging around to avoid dropping the vegetable piles.

Our cold room is freezing cold. I turn on the electrical cutter; the sound of it freezes in the air. In the washing room, the water is running and there's a smell of disinfectant. It is my shift at the cutting and shredding section. It is Jenny's shift in the cleaning room and it is Big Jimmy who, as usual, helps us with moving big boxes around.

Big Jimmy brings boxes of carrots. I empty half of them; the shapes and the colours of vegetables are part of my dreams and nightmares. Constantly I see long vegetables and round vegetables. As I cut them, the carrots and cabbages blow their smelly breath into the air. Where do these smells come from? Do vegetables have some place inside them which, as soon as we cut them, releases their smell?

'Jenny, what is it?'

'Ah, this *VO*.'

She runs to the toilet.

Barry, with his massive body, is moving cartoons of chlorine and washing liquid. I am supposed to work with him.

He pushes me and I fall. 'Get out, stupid. I don't want to see you.'

I ignore him and run the water; I empty a box of carrots but then I can't do more – my fingers feel as if they are nails.

As soon as Jenny comes in, Barry leaves his work and runs towards her.

'Jimmy, Jimmy.'

Jimmy comes to help me first. Then he goes after him.

The floor is wet, both big sinks are overflowing and some shredded vegetables are spread on the floor. Jimmy reaches Barry and pulls him from the back, hooking his fingers into Barry's belt. But Barry twists his big body and releases himself and pulls Jimmy's pants. Jimmy holds on to the bench corner; resisting; the floor is slick but he avoids slipping by planting his feet firmly on the wet floor, like a calf planting its hooves on the ground. He smashes Barry with his elbow; Barry's nose bleeds and he slips on the wet floor. Tap water from different basins overflows and the chopped cabbages and carrots come dancing out.

I shout, 'Stop it. Stop it. I will call the police.'

Barry leaves the room. Jimmy totters over the sliced vegetables and goes to the locker room.

In the tea room, I see Jenny.

'I am sick all the time. You know, looking at any carrot or cabbage makes me to vomit – the shapes, ah, and this smell. The vegetable smells disgust me. I even have nightmares about vegetables. The other night, I saw myself running and dancing in the desert. It was the Sahara, hot, orange, lonely and mesmerised. But I was happy, dancing, barefoot. There is a person who plays a flute. When I look back, I see my husband, Barry and Abdollah are coming after me in the shape of carrots, the sound of a flute is coming from their carrots. I ran away from them. A wind takes a bunch of sand and dances with it, rolling up and down.

On a horizon of my mirage, silver white, I give birth to a baby. The baby soon turns to a mermaid and disappears in the sand and this repeats again. All the shapes and smells make me feel sick.'

I leave the room.

'What do I do? I am scared,' she shouts after me.

'You are in a mess, Jenny, you are in a mess.'

*

He puts his dream on the breakfast table in the kitchen; piles of folders; and his tape recorder. He listens to his voice recorder and takes notes. I look at the business record of the restaurant: the cost, the profit, the successful events which have been advertised in the local Fairfield newspaper and on the Liverpool and Fairfield community radio.

'How many interviews do you have?'

'Fifteen so far.'

'All are Iranians?'

'No, eight of them are Afghani.' He drinks a bottle of water in one go and looks at me. The eyes of his dreams shine in his voice – a sweet giggle.

'You know, I really liked their lifestyle. I am thinking maybe we should change our life too.'

'You mean we buy a farm and live as farmers?'

'Why not?'

'Because we are not farmers and we don't know anything about farming.' I drink a glass of water.

'We don't know anything about restaurants but you are considering buying a restaurant!'

'I am buying a business. I will only supervise the business. Jimmy, Jenny and Jimmy's brother will run the restaurant and all of them are experienced people.' A red dot of agitation comes to my throat.

'You should trust me with this.'

The moment passes like a chunk of metal.

'I trust you with your community radio project.'

'I know – I know you do. But I am tired of waiting for one day when I will or will not be a successful radio producer.' He stares at my hands; the smell of gel mixes with the boiling sound of water. He turns off the kettle. The tears of two tea bags evaporate in the air.

'We can buy a vegetable farm, it could be cheaper. Some of those farmers I saw only grow vegetables.'

I smile at his suggestion. 'What do you want to call your project?'

'Fresh Food People.'

'You can't.'

The smell of fresh brewed tea is mixed with the fragrance of carrot and cabbage in my mind.

*

I lie down on my son's bed, massaging my hands with Voltaren gel. The smell is a ghost. His room smells of the fish tank. I can hear fish talk merging and submerging in the tank. The small blue lights of the tank make his posters visible: Australian Socceroo team, Tim Cahill with ball in hands. Bob Marley and Che on the other wall. Where are the girls? Or boys? They should be somewhere? Curious, I look around; flipping aside his bed sheets and pillows.

I open a drawer. My spider fingers lock.

'Dinner is ready.'

The invitation arrives from the walls. No girls, no boys.

A Clear Darkness

Day one

We left the house in Zahedan, the house which had been provided by
the *Ghachagchi*.

'You will fly from Tehran to Zahedan. Make sure you don't pack too
much – that attracts the security guard's attention. Get a small bag only
for your child.' He turned to me. 'You don't wear sneakers or any kind
of sport shoes. That attracts attention. Wear a pair of women's shoes.'

We had been in hiding in the home of relatives for about seven days.
Until the last night before we said goodbye to our family, nobody knew
where we were.

We made the deal in Tehran, four days before our departure. Reza, my
husband's brother-in-law, negotiated with the *Ghachagchi*. We were sitting
in his living room, windows covered with black paper, all the lights off. It
was curfew. Our baby son was asleep, his ears blocked with cotton balls to
shield him from the sound of bombing. We were sitting in candlelight.

Reza said, 'I will give you half of the money. When you send them
to the other side, I will pay you the rest. You have to bring their ID
documents here and give them to me after they have used them in the
UN office in Quetta.'

'I was terrified. I was just pretending to be strong. I was worried
how he would handle you,' he told us years later.

We slept in this empty house for two nights. Each night, we put
our son to sleep wrapped in a blanket, but we stayed awake. 'Where
are we?' I asked my husband stupidly. We had been brought there in
the early morning.

He had bought his way by paying some local policemen; an amount
he did not reveal. *'Mohem nist.'*

We didn't see the city, if there was any of the city left. Most of the cities in the south were evacuated during the war.

When we arrived at Zahedan airport, a man who we recognised from the description given to us in Tehran – '…khaki jacket, he will be holding a green plastic bag…' – picked us up.

We arrived at a house in a dusty narrow street.

The first three days in Zahedan

I made tea three times but we didn't drink any of it. The water was muddy and impure.

'*Nakhor.* You might get cholera.'

We boiled the water five times and filtered it with my scarf to make formula for our son. Luckily we bought a can of Baby Boy on the black market just before we left Tehran. We also bought three packets of five dummies – our son didn't sleep without his dummy – and sleeping drops we got from our paediatrician. I bought ten packets of Winston cigarettes; I wouldn't survive without them.

And then on the evening of the third day, a man came to the door. We drove in the heart of the night. The Baluchi man's voice was young but he looked old. I sat on his motorbike holding my baby, making sure he had his dummy.

'Make sure your baby doesn't cry on the way, the desert air echoes everywhere,' the *Ghachagchi* told us before we left Tehran.

My husband sat behind me.

The Baluchi was driving like a storm. 'I have to go fast. There are security guards all the way and they know the roads very well.'

The ride was on sandy roads toward the desert. We were riding towards the wind in the morning, sightless, directionless; towards the endless, towards the winds, storms and sand.

Day four

We reached a dirt-floored, cave-like dwelling. The motorbike rider opened the door with a big key. The door rattled and opened inwards.

The room was dark and its earthen floor was covered with a small straw mattress. In one corner there was bedding. There was a built-in triangle-shaped clay shelf. Under the shelf there was a clay water jar.

'*Ab onja hast.* Someone will bring food.'

Whatever we asked him, he just shrugged. 'Someone will tell you.'

I checked the water jar – it was full and it was odourless. I put my finger in it and tasted the water; clean, fresh. After almost four days without proper food and water, even a sip seemed to soak my whole body. We washed our son's face and hands. From beneath a mask of sand, our child emerged.

My husband went outside.

I sat beside my son for a while. The water, the smell of moisture, was playing with my mind. I touched the body of the clay jug. The coolness of it scared me; I felt the coolness of a cemetery, as if my ghost had bathed me. Here in the desert, everything felt like it had a double, a ghost which was coming with us side by side.

Where did this water come from? With its palanquin of ghosts? Who brought it here? I looked outside through a small hole. There was just dust and hills. Where is the world?

We didn't know where we were. We just knew that we were riding deeper and deeper into no-man's-land. It was as if the desert was deaf to all that was happening in the country. While in the south-west the war was tearing the country, here in the south-east we were far from the war.

'*Yeki dareh miad,*' my husband said and quickly shut the door and stood behind it.

We were shaking. We were in the middle of nowhere and someone was coming towards us.

It was the bike rider. He came in and there were two young men with him.

They introduced themselves. X was from the north province and Y was from the capital city.

My husband and I looked at each other suspiciously; we didn't talk much to each other. Talk was dangerous, so we decided, like the desert, to be and act as if we were deaf.

The only question was, 'Where are you going?'

'To Pakistan.'

At least we all had one destination in mind.

The bike rider brought some goat's milk and bread. 'We will move early in the morning, four a.m. Do you have a watch?'

'Areh.' My husband set the alarm.

We started as a caravan of motorbikes this time. After a few days in the cave, the midnight air felt chilly. There wasn't any wind, as if it had been locked away by an invisible power.

'Where are we going? Do I need to take water?' I asked, feeling terrified to leave the water behind.

'Yekam vardar. Not much. We'll give you water on the way,' the bike rider said.

I took the water flask and suddenly jumped. There was a small lizard; she moved fast toward the clay wall, turned back and stared at my face. She had a dirt-coloured face. I looked at her limbs. I remembered my nightmares while pregnant seeing small lizards with cut off legs and hands. She tapped her little tail on the wall and danced away. I filled up the water flask and made fresh milk in the bottle. I didn't know that this would be our last water before we reached a real desert.

Rooz-e- panjoom

We arrived at a nomad camp in the evening. Through the road dust, a tent appeared like the open wings of a bat. Our backs were stiff from the long dusty ride. The motorbike driver carried my small bag. Two men were sitting around a small fire; there were two camels and a few goats sitting around them. There was a smell of burnt milk in the air. Around them there were bundles of colourful kilim saddle-carpets and salt bags of the same fabric. Those weather-beaten faces received us with no words but one of them moved the bundles to the other side of the camels. After showing us to our place, they returned to the same spot and did nothing. They sat around the fire and minded the boiling water. Every now and then, they looked at each other and carried on baking bread and making tea. One of them handed us tea, in red plastic cups.

My husband had a sip and spat it. 'It is not tea, *shoreh.*'

We whispered to make sure we didn't offend them, unaware of the fact that these two Baluchi didn't understand Farsi at all.

'*Bokhor,* they are watching us.'

We drank the bitterness of the tea.

'Anyway, we shouldn't be far from Pakistan. Not long to the UN door.'

That gave us hope, remembering that we were not on this salt odyssey for a holiday; we were fugitives, running away from persecution. But somehow we felt safe here. I hadn't felt safe since the revolution started, since war started, since I had been imprisoned for two years for believing in a secular society, for being a member of the left party in Iran. My husband was avoiding being drafted into the war.

The dusty floor of the tent was covered with Baluchi rugs, all red and blue. We sat on the mat, leaving our baby on a small mattress.

The bike driver disappeared, and then he returned through the dust like an arrow. He left the baby's water flask on the floor and dusted away into the air again. We didn't notice him when he came back, we were too tired to see or hear or feel anything. We were glad that we had arrived somewhere, anywhere.

Here, in this spot, war seemed mountains away. Time didn't run forwards or backwards here. Time was half air, half stone. I could lead myself into it and feel safe. Here, I could put my son to sleep on the arm of a big stone without blocking his ears with cotton balls. This place was soundless, silent, and deaf to all the problems in Tehran.

These Baluchi: I wanted to trust them but I had no idea what they were thinking and they seemed to be thinking all the time. I imagined their thoughts just passed through their minds as the wind passed through the camp.

Soon, the darkness eclipsed us. The nomads moved away from the dim fire and went to their blankets. We were supposed to sleep on the body of two very large stones. The scenery at night became even stranger; we couldn't say whether we were in the hills or flat land. It seemed a mirage. During the day, sun seemed to empty the entire landscape. It was a bone-coloured landscape. It seemed that everything had a great weight and mass except the weather. It was the second month of spring, early days in April – the air was thin. Then the moonlight came; in the heart of the blue sky, the land waved in front of my eyes – a quality of water and stone.

My husband slept next to our son. I couldn't sleep. I lit a cigarette and inhaled deeply. It made me dizzy and sleepy.

I looked at the sky, the massive black blue. A clear darkness outlined it. The world starts here and never ends, I thought. I felt that my head was merged into the salty sand, then I could see the Ghouls coming, arriving from every corner in the desert, passing tall stones and reaching us, reaching my baby. They were licking my baby's feet; they licked and licked till his body disappeared. I screamed and woke up to huge eyes with long eyelashes. My heart was pumping, my body was shaking. I then realised I was staring at a camel.

There were two new nomads, older than the other two. We looked around. There was no sign of the first two. These two new nomads' Farsi was even more limited than the other two. They made it clear to us with a few broken sentences that we had to pack and go. But first we had to eat.

'Who are these people? Where are the other two?' I whispered to my husband.

'I don't know. I was asleep when they came.'

We had eaten the same food for the past four days: doughy bread and goat's milk. We fed our son with his formula. The strong sun, hunger and the fluidity of people made us suspicious.

'Where is our man?' My husband asked.

'*Balayeh koheh*,' answered the nomad who looked much older than the other. While answering, he pointed to the peak of the mountain in the far away location.

'He is on the other side of this mountain? Is he in Pakistan?' my husband asked.

'No, up there, he is there, up. Up. Up is Pakistan.'

His answer infuriated us. Both of us were mountain climbers and had been on many mountain journeys during our university years. We knew that when you climb a mountain you have to walk down to get to the land on the other side but this Baluchi man was trying to convince us that if we went up the mountain we would be in Pakistan and find flat land.

While our questioning was getting nowhere, we saw one of the previous Baluchis approach.

'Now, who are these people?' I whispered.

'Who are these people?' My husband questioned the Baluchi in a corner. 'Where is our guide?'

'He will meet you soon,' the Baluchi said with the same calm as before.

'You are putting us in danger. We don't know who these people are. We were meant to be in Pakistan two days ago.'

'Yes, the plan has changed.'

We didn't know what the original plan was anyway. We only knew that we had to pay the smuggler to take us to Pakistan in three days and show us the office of United Nations. But we had now been stranded in the mountains with a group of old Baluchi guides who didn't speak Farsi and we didn't know where exactly they were taking us.

'You have to go.'

The younger Baluchi helped the other two to bring two camels. They made the camels kneel down. My husband sat first then he held our baby and then I sat. Then the sudden movement of the camel scared us and when the camel stood up, we slid down. The water flask hit the ground and broke. Our baby woke up and started screaming.

'*Saketesh kon*,' three of them ordered in panicked, angry voices.

What we managed to understand from their broken Farsi was that

we were surrounded by snipers and near a police station. My husband
gave a few sleeping drops to our son and put a dummy in his mouth.
That made him quiet.

We had to try to get on the back of the camel again. We learnt that
when camels want to stand up, they raise themselves onto their front
feet first, and then their hind legs, and we had to move backward and
then forward as the camel rose. The Baluchi assumed everybody knew
how to ride camels and didn't bother to teach us the basics. This time,
they put saddles on the animals.

Day six

We rode through darkness. The swift-footed animals seemed to be
swimming into the softness of the desert sand. We couldn't see
anything; we could only feel the animals' wavy movement. On a few
occasions, the nomads stopped the camels and ordered us to hold on
to the animal's bridle and force them to sit.

We sat behind them, hiding from unknown danger which we could-
n't see but the Baluchi could smell. The old Baluchi had a sense of sound
sharper than any animal. It was amazing how they could hear anything
in such wind.

There is a seasonal wind in Sistan and Baluchistan. The wind we
were crossing through was Levar. '*Levareh, levareh,*' the old man was
telling us. It was dry and dusty. Even in a headscarf, I could breathe the
dryness of the air, sharp inside my nostrils. We were luckily not going
through the Gav-kosh, which was so severe that even Sahara bulls could
not survive it. There are also the north or Gurish winds and western or
Gard winds. Nomads believe that winds fight with one another sometimes; if two winds from north and west meet, their spirits will get upset
and cause a deadly storm.

Each time they heard the danger and ordered us to stop and hide,
there was some car passing on a faraway road. We only could see the
car's lights as a slice of clear line in the horizon.

In the light of a new day, we finally stopped.

'We have to rest. We can't move in daylight. It is dangerous.' The older nomad made us understand this.

The wind had stopped. They guided us to gather around the camels and eat; this time, only yeasty bread and no milk or water. Unlike the other Baluchi, these older Baluchi didn't slice the bread. They just passed it to us. Each of us had to take a bite of it and pass it to the next person. We understood that breaking bread was wastful because it created crumbs. Everything here was a whole: whole bread, whole milk, whole time, and whole space, nothing in slices or pieces.

We didn't sleep all night as we were still hungry. Soon, the nomads were snoring, cocooned in their blankets. The camels had stopped moaning; the dromedaries were ready for loading. The two Baha'i boys were resting too. I looked at the sky, massive blue, and calm. A clear darkness outlined it.

By my side, my husband and son went to sleep too. The early morning daylight seemed silvery. In the silence of the day, somehow you could hear the rhythm of things unseen around you. Why couldn't I sleep? My heart was thumping. Where was the world now? It looked like an upside-down ocean. It was as if all the shades of blue had been used to create it. The world starts here and never ends, I thought.

Day seven

Our son is asleep again. He rarely wakes. We don't know if this is good or bad. We worry that the sleeping drops affect his health but if he wakes up, he will be hungry and we don't have water to make milk for him.

We are trying to make a tent with some of our clothes to protect our son from the sun and from the influx of flies which swim in the air or sit on our son's face. In an environment so barren and empty, a plague of flies. It is as if the flies smell us.

The two Baha'i boys are lying down on stones, facing the sky, soaking heat into their bodies. 'If you sit under the sun, gradually your body get used to it and you don't feel the heat. You even don't feel thirsty any more.'

Our smugglers left us in this desert to go and find their leader. I stare at the abstract landscape of the Taftan Mountain. The salty stones stand out from the heart of the earth. One thing I can't understand is the lack of shade. Even behind the tall stones, it is difficult to hide from the sun. My gaze is getting hazy and I am unsure if it is from dehydration or just pure exhaustion. I see something colourful move. It is as tall as the stone.

Four of us watch it: a mass of coloured flesh. Each time she moves her head, she morphs from yellowish-green into ochre. It looks like pre-historic, a salamander. She runs away. She is a fugitive too.

Our son wakes up, crying, screaming from hunger. I hold him. He feels smaller and thinner in my arms. His beautiful face looks thinner, his body turns red from sunburn. I try to calm him down but there is no chance. His sharp voice cuts through the stones.

Three Baluchi approach.

'Make him quiet, make him quiet.' The older man, shaking his arms, rushes towards us.

'*Baluchi kesafat ahmagh*, I will kill you. He is hungry, do you understand, you old idiot? We don't have water to make milk for him. Where are you taking us? Where is your leader? You are killing us, you are killing my baby.' I rush towards him.

My husband and the two Baha'i boys run towards me, trying to calm me down. I sit on the edge of a stone, exhausted, too tired to cry.

Then we watch the old Baluchi walk around to find water. He walks and assesses the soil first with his feet and then he kneels and listens. He checks a few places and then he shouts to us. The three Baluchi dig.

The water is thick and muddy. I run and take some into a small jar the Baluchi give me. I use my scarf and filter it into the milk bottle. I repeat it many times but it is still dark. The white powdered milk disappears into the darkness of the liquid.

My husband rushes to me, '*Nadeh behesh*. He will get sick. He will get cholera.' He drags the bottle from my hand.

The Baluchi leave us again, supposedly to bring our leader. The baby is screaming, shouting. His throat is weak and the sound of his crying is scratchier, weaker.

'Please feed him. At least he won't die from starvation. I don't care if he gets sick. I can't tolerate this any more.'

One of the Baha'i boys loses his patience and snatches the bottle from my husband's hand and puts it into my son's mouth.

Our son drinks the muddy milk. He becomes quiet. His bottle is empty. He is quiet and he becalms the desert storm. Sand and stones return to their places. The sun stays in the middle of the sky. And the desert sky holds the sun as if she is her own quiet baby.

Day eight

We are walking slowly behind the old man. He is walking turtle-like and then suddenly I notice that my shoe is broken.

I stop and yell at him, '*Vaysta*.'

He stops and turns toward us. My husband tries to fix my shoe; there is not enough material on my summer shoes to be used as an extra part. Gradually, he gives up, so do I. We move again. Two Baluchi in the front, my husband and baby after them, I am in the third row, behind me two Baha'i boys and at the rear the other Baluchi.

The scenery is changing; it is as if finally we are coming out of the end of the world. There are different shapes of stones, there are tall rocks and cliffs, there are shades, but still the air has a salty aroma.

Soon, we reach a cliff which has a passage; we are happy, as we think this is our way.

Two Baluchi stop and whisper to each other.

'No, we have to continue.'

'*Tondtar rah bia*. We have to get to the passage before dark. Otherwise, we will get lost.'

His words soothe me; he talks as if he really cares and knows the way. I follow his order; carry my shoe in my hand. At the edge of another cliff, a bag with pieces of clothes around it is left open.

We walk in silence; adapting to the everyday rhythm of terror, the feeling of being watched. Every now and then, the older Baluchi turns round and watches us. My steps are slower than before. My feet blister.

My husband insists that I wear his shoes but that doesn't work; his shoes are too big for me.

We walk up the mountain till late afternoon. Then we cross a plateau.

In the late afternoon, we reach a place which looks like a valley. They stop, we stop.

The older Baluchi checks the surroundings, moves around and says, 'Here, we have to go up.'

I look at the point he is pointing at. It is a tall cliff, smooth, without any notch or split or crack. Four of us look at each other in shock.

'How are we supposed to go up there?' one of the boys asks.

'*Rah boro*,' the old Baluchi says while showing with his finger that we should walk and climb up the rock.

My husband hands me our son. The warmness of his body pleases me even in this heat. I kiss his calm and beautiful face. His real smell emerges from the smell of sand and salt. The smell of his face reminds me why I am here.

The two boys and my husband check the cliff. They walk around it, touch it try to find a way to go up. There is no chance.

'We can't do it,' my husband says.

'*Bayad beyid*,' the Baluchi says, staring at my husband.

'How are we supposed to take our baby?' I ask him.

'*Bache man mibaram, ba tanab*,' he says, searching for something.

I drop my baby into my husband's arm and rush to the old man. '*Baluchi's kesafat, as dastet zeleh shodam*. You Baluchi, you don't under-stand anything. You want to hang my baby. I kill you.' And cry.

And he doesn't understand me; the only Farsi word he picks up was the word kill. He says,'I am Baluch.' And he means no one can touch him.

'I am Turkish. When you sleep, I kill you.'

My husband tries to calm me down and talk to them but I have lost my trust in them, lost my ability to remain calm and think. I can't walk any more and I start believing that perhaps they are lying to us. I am shouting, my husband shouting at the old man, those two boys are shouting at the other Baluchi, we all are shouting.

'I am not moving from here any more. Who are these people? We don't know them. Maybe they are lying to us. *Hamineh, tamom shod digeh, man nemiam.* I will sit here till he comes.' I take my son from my husband.

He doesn't resist. He walks away.

I sit at a corner, slowly put my son on a flat piece of land. I refuse to move. The others follow me. Three Baluchi leave us and disappear down the bottom of the hill.

We sit close to each other. It is late afternoon; the sun is setting behind mountains. My foot hurts; my big toenail is torn and bleeding. I sit on the edge of stone; somehow, the stone doesn't feel hard any more. In front of me, I can see yellow and green patterns; perhaps we are getting closer to our destination, maybe we are in Pakistan. At that time, I didn't know that I was actually looking at Iran. I was sitting in the opposite direction to our endless pilgrimage to the unknown.

The air soothes my blood; a lump of blood coagulated on my toe has a thousand pulses. The air here has a gentleness which acts on my toe as if it is narcotic, soothing.

My husband puts our baby on his legs, make his legs the baby's rocking cradle. They both sleep. Their exhausted faces look so similar. I touch their faces. Neither of them moves. The two other boys are asleep too. I am the only one who is awake.

Midnight

One of the boys is fed up with waiting, 'I will try to go a little bit further down from the cliff to see what is there and if there is any other way.' He disappears.

Early in the morning, we hear some voices. *'Zaneh divaneh.* They can shoot you right there from far away.' It is him, our guy, the *Ghachagchi* we met in Tehran; he appears like the ghost of the mountain's breath. He walks towards me with a smile, and another young man is following him. 'This is my cousin.' He doesn't give us his name.

'Where have you been? What is going on? Why are we still in here?'

'Move, we have to go, I tell you on the way. Where you are sitting now is the most dangerous place. They can see us. You have passed the correct passage. It is further down.'

'Are we still in Iran?'

'Yes.'

He goes to my husband. His face changes when he looks at my son. All of a sudden, he acts like a child, making faces for my son to make him laugh. My son sits in the arms of this stranger comfortably, his eyes puffy, his face puffy from crying and sleeping.

Our walk now is measured and slow.

He is looking around all the time. 'I had to change your plan. There were many arrests.'

We have another a few hours of arduous journey; the land has a salty smell.

He stops and says, '*Az inja.* We go from here.'

The next road we have to walk through is not horizontal. It is a chasm, a massive birth canal, bordered by two enormous cliffs. We have to climb the chasm to reach the land of Pakistan. The leader takes my son with him, moves up as if he is a goat that is born in this mountain. I follow next. I climb one step after him, using the same cracks and small holes he uses. Every now and then, I stick in the narrow gap in the cliffs; I stop and look down. I see my husband, struggling as I do, and beyond the shape of his body, there are two Baha'i and then an endless open air. I am exhausted and my shoulders are numb from pressing against the cliffs.

Finally, I hear the *Ghachagchi* shout, '*Be Pakistan khosh omadid.*'

His welcome for us is a vanload of Pakistani mandarins, biscuits and Fanta. We are surprised, looking at the flatness of the land after climbing the cliff. We eat endlessly.

'*Yavash yavash, mariz mishid.*' He tries to warn us about our eating but our hunger and thirst seems endless.

My son drinks real milk. We shower our faces with clean water from the tank he has in the back of the van.

When we are done with eating, drinking and cleaning, he sends the van away and a white Paykan, an Iranian version of a Ford, comes.

'We have to go.' He sits in the passenger seat next to the driver and four of us are in the back seat.

He drives very fast. He gives us all a scarf. The scenery is all salt, a white ocean. Even with the windows up, still salt filters into the car. Our car is the only thing in this vast and broad road. Its cracks snake the landscape. I can see my husband's eyelashes and eyebrows are white; my eyes burn. My son starts crying, he has wet himself and I don't have anything to change him.

The car stops in front of a white clay shack. We get out of the car. Our muscles are too stiff to walk. We duck inside the entrance, descend two steps, find ourselves inside a cave. There are a few freezers on the floor.

The smuggler takes out a coca cola and tells us, '*Bardarid.*'

The *Ghachagchi* gives me a new scarf. I wrap my son with the scarf – no nappy, no pants, just the scarf.

We ride again, through this white nightmare. Our eyes are burning. Inside the car, the air conditioner blows hot. I ask to open the windows but he says that is dangerous.

Before dark, we reach an empty plateau.

He stops the car and says, '*Esterahat mikonim.*'

We get out of the car and take off our scarves. Our faces are masked with salt. I feel the air, the coolness of her, but this breeze scares me, she says something; she tells me she is unbound.

Taking Care of Eggs

1

The child would sit with her sister to paint eggs for *Haft Sin* for Nowrooz. Their mother had thought them this. The *Haft Sin* table was set with seven items, beginning with the letter *sin* (S); *Sib, Samanoo, Sabzi, Sekeh, Sumac, Serkeh* and *Sir* – and there were also painted eggs, a mirror and a fishbowl with goldfish.

When she was only five, the family left the land of Nowrooz, and went to the faraway land of Oz, where there were Xmas and Easter holidays. They were living in a farmhouse in the town of Campbell and when Nowrooz came, there wasn't any sign of it in Sin City. Still her father let her and her older sister paint eggs for their very small *Haft Sin.*

When Nowrooz finished, Easter came and her father bought them small chocolate eggs, the size of quail eggs. He mainly hid them in the kitchen, where there was enough room to hide chocolate eggs. She started hiding chocolate eggs inside shoes and in the kitchen pots. When Easter finished, she hid the shoes. Every morning when her father was preparing to go to work, he had to go to the kitchen to find his shoes – in the kitchen pots or cabinet.

One day, the little girl sat in the kitchen for a long time, quietly, stirring a pair of shoes in the pot. When her father asked her jokingly what she was cooking, she said she was cooking shoe eggs.

One morning, her father had trouble finding his shoes. 'Where are my shoes?' he asked his little girl. 'I need to wear them and go to work.'

'They hatched their eggs and all of them went out of the door as a family. They went back to the land of Nowrooz.'

2

There was a man who used to go to cockfights when he was a little boy. In the afternoons, the proud trainers sent their fighters into the cockpit. The little boy witnessed the savage roosters fanning their neck feathers and whirling their wings as they jumped and parried at one another, striking at each other with feet and beaks.

There were bets placed and disputes over the payments. In stalled contests, the owners would rush and yank at the birds' beaks. Some owners held them beak-to-beak. In those moments, the crowd shouted, whistled, clapped to excite the birds even more. The audience – the village people – made gestures with their faces in front of the roosters; some scowled, some moved on one leg and some made voices as if they were roosters themselves. Those who bet the most shouted the loudest. The women and girls in the village watched the games from far away from the main circle. Unlike the men and boys who constantly whistled and shouted, the women and girls just watched the game quietly while looking after the kids or older people.

When he was much younger, and the height of the audience didn't allow him the chance to see the fight, he and his friends played with his tin train. The little boys ran around and the dust of the dried land rose from the ground after them. Every now and then, they stopped when the audience whistled or shouted or sang like roosters. They did as the grown-ups did; they shouted and sang like roosters.

The fights didn't finish until one rooster was dead or covered in his last drops of blood. The dead birds or half-dead birds were discarded into a barrel. And then the crowd dispersed; the owners, organisers and those who won or lost money left earlier than the rest of the crowd, before the bribed law officers drank and smoked away the bribes, and demanded more money for cigarettes and beer. Those owners whose birds were considered good enough to heal again for another fight were cared for by the owner, and their blood was scrubbed off their bodies, wounds were stitched, and ointments applied. The atmosphere in the village remained in dusty excitement and ferocious calm until the next game.

3

As a young man, my father migrated to a country where cockfighting was illegal. He bought a small chicken farm in the west of Sin City.

When I became ten, I helped my sister Lili collect the eggs. Every day before we went to school, we had to check the nesting boxes for their eggs. Then we slid the handles back and let the chooks free in the garden. We had five hens' coops called the Taj Mahal. Numbers 1 and 2 were my responsibility. I was in charge of three Silkies. My father gave me this responsibility because they were docile and broody. I had to move them to collect their creamy eggs. I liked holding them and touching their soft feathers. They sat quietly in my arms when I kissed their walnut combs. Lili was in charge of the other three coops. Lili had two Death Clucks in one coop. They were totally black; even their inner organs were black. In coop 4, she had two Coronation Sussex with lavender-grey feathers. The last one was a cockerel. Ever since he was little, he was aggressive, so our father decided to keep him away from the others in number 5.

The chicken farm was far away from our main home, to keep the house free from chicken smells, but still everything in the house smelled of feathers, eggs and hay. At school, most of the children didn't play with us because they said we stank. So Lili and I kept to ourselves; our chickens were our playmates. We had names for them. Mine were Divine, Cipher and Hope. My sister had Sage, Enigma, Thunder and Venture. The last one, a rooster, was named by our father; this one was our father's favourite. He used to say it was the son he never had. He called him Khoroos Jangi, and for short we called him just Jangi.

Every day, Lili and I poured the poultry pellets into the dispensers before going to school. They loved Golden Grain layer pellets my father bought from Woolworths. Lili and I created our own chook chat and songs, such as singalong, cluckalong. We sang while we fed them. In the afternoons when we let the birds run around the garden, we sang our singalong, cluckalong, and those birds translated them into walk around and nibbled through wheat and corn which were scattered all around the farm. And when we were together, three of us without birds, Lili and I used to sing our songs. We both knew that it meant I have to tell you something but you should promise me don't tell Daddy.

One day, Lili showed me an ibis tattooed on her backside; the body didn't look like the bird, but the down-curved beak was done perfectly. Lili had crush on Ms Donovan, her science teacher. We both sang that day for a bird who didn't sing back to us.

4

Our father said, 'Keep the tins, girls.'

We did.

When he had time, he made a hole in the bottom of Campbell soup cans, and passed a string through them. He said while lining up a few empty tins, 'In my village, one tin could go a long way. My mother used it to keep dried beans and she also used some as plant pots. We always grew our mint and basil in the tin. Those days, when I was a young boy, food in my village was as rare as hen's teeth.'

Lili and I mainly ate canned food, Campbell soup and canned beans. We were not allowed to use the stove. Every day, Lili emptied canned food and heated it up in the microwave. But some Sundays, our father cooked for us. Lili and I walked around him and told him about every one of our hens, their behaviour and their eggs. He cooked the cracked eggs which he couldn't sell in the market. The smell of the cooking oil and eggs was so good. We always thought we were eating such a variety of foods but all was egg, egg, egg. He named the food according to the hen who laid the egg. Egg with tomato and mint he called Divine or Cipher or Hope omelette. Egg with butter and cheese he called Enigma, Thunder and Sage. He named the scrambled eggs Daddy.

While cooking, he used to say, 'C'mon, Lili, you should learn how to cook. You are a big girl now.' But he never let us get close to the gas stove.

One day, Lili pushed and kicked my tin train. She was stronger than I, but I didn't give up; I pulled her hair. She shouted.

'Damn it, cut it out, you two. Stop it right now,' he called from the bathroom, where he was shaving.

We stopped. He looked at his face in the mirror and wiped the blood from his neck. When he kissed us before he went to work, I saw the wound was still wet.

'Don't fight. Take care of the eggs.'

5

Jangi, even when he was little, chased my sister after she fed the birds, and as soon as she turned back, Jangi followed her and pecked her hand so severely it bled. In a month or two, we noticed that he had spurs on the back of his legs, and he started racing in the garden across the yard and chasing the other birds.

Whenever our father had time, he played with Jangi, teasing him by pulling his tail or provoking him by running after him. Jangi was always agile and ready to fight. As Jangi got older, he became heavier; the red fleshy skin under his beak. My father chased him while singing like him, 'Goo goo li goo goo.' Jangi sang back to him, 'Goo goo li goo goo.' Sometimes, my father showed Jangi the food, and as the bird reached the food, my father pulled it away and made Jangi chase him around the backyard. Sometimes, he locked the bird's legs and rooted him in the dirt next to our only banksia tree. Lili and I cried but father closed his ears. When my father eventually fed Jangi, the rooster would stop eating and looked at my father with calm, as if imploring him not to do it again. For a few days, Jangi's morning song was different. His goo goo li goo goo wasn't as loud as it was in every dawn. He wasn't singing to wake up the day, but singing his liturgy. Soon, the time of his salvation would end and everything would start all over again. But it was Jangi who always won the fight.

While feeding him, my father would say, 'I envy him.'

One day, he placed a big mirror against the wall in Jangi's coop.

6

One day when we came back from school, we found our backyard covered with dead birds, sun-dried egg yolks, blood and hens' feathers.

In some places, the egg white was already dried by the air and the sun's heat. Some egg yolks were smeared and, in some parts, eggs were cracked and undamaged egg yolks were out of the shell as if they were sunflowers that had just bloomed. Feathers, grey, white, blue, yellow and red were tangled in the trees. Divine and Page had broken wings, Cipher had no claw and I couldn't see where Hope was. I was just shouting and searching for my lost friends. Lili was crying and holding her Sage and Enigma. Thunder and Venture, with blood-covered bodies, were at her side. There was a crack on the mirror and it was covered with blood. Feathers covered the ground around Jangi's body like the autumn leaves of a persimmon tree. Then we heard our father's truck, stopped outside the gate.

7

He walked in, step by step, looking at the ground. He reached Jangi's body. He kneeled in front of him, patted his head. He then looked at the mirror. For a while, he stared at the blood. He gently touched the cracked corner of the mirror and quietly said, 'The bird in the mirror crossed Jangi.' He sat on the ground and held the dead body of Jangi in his arm.

Laundry Day

Lili piled a heavy white sheet onto her shoulder, pulling it from the wicker basket she'd dragged from the laundry to the clothesline in the backyard. She stood on tiptoes, struggling to reach the clothesline. She heaved the sheet over the thick wire her husband had fixed to the wall of the courtyard and stretched the sheet taut so she wouldn't have to iron it when she brought it in. Already she could feel drops of sweat budding on her back.

It was day three of the heatwave and it seemed that the sun's rays were on the sky even at nights. She stepped back and stared at the washed white sheet, then she stepped in close again, examining the fabric with her fingers, where she thought the bloodstain was. She could smell bleach. There wasn't any sign of the blood. Since her last miscarriage two month ago, her period was heavier than ever.

She bent down and took the second heavy sheet on her shoulder. The sun hot on her back. The sheet soaking her thin T-shirt. Lili stood, pulling the weight of the sheet from her, lost in the light and the mixed lemon fragrance of No Frills washing powder and bleach, the feeling of the sheet against her arms like damp skin. When she stood up again, she screamed and stepped back. There, behind the sheet, the shape of a body pressed into the fabric. Long thighs, a belly and the lace of a beige bra patterned the sheet.

Lili stared, her heart pounding and then she looked to the house from the corner of her eyes. All the windows were open. The white lace curtains were swaying with a gentle breeze. Her husband wasn't home and the house was empty. But she glimpsed eyes through parted curtains. She felt all the windows were watching. In the silence of hot air, she could smell the tang of green tomatoes coming from their farm.

The shape moved deeper into the fabric and wrapped her body into it, the wooden pegs stuck to some corners.

'Isn't it too hot, Mother?' It was Shifteh, Lili's stepdaughter. The stepdaughter picked up a cage from the corner of the laundry and walked back into the house, Lili's mouth open like an empty dam dreaming of water.

Lili dropped the plastic washtub at the door step of the laundry, pushed away some spiderwebs hanging from the laundry door, and ran up the path back to the house. In bare feet, she could feel the hot over-grown grass sleeping, sinking then rising under her feet.

Lili walked inside; a damp, moist darkness had built up in the hall-way. The bird must have been freed from her cage. She couldn't see her but she could smell her. After a while, the darkness made itself clear. Shifteh lay on the living room sofa still in her beige bra and undies, drinking a beer. Her suntanned body was spread on the old yellow vel-vet sofa. She was moving one of her legs as if a pendulum. Her layers of anklets were jingling. Her green coloured parrot was standing on the coffee table staring at Lili. When Shifteh touched the parrot, the bird did a small move. The stepdaughter put the bird on her head and then drained her beer and dropped the empty can on Lili's knitting basket and walked down the hall. She stopped at the bathroom door and grinned at her stepmother, then went into the bathroom and shut the door.

Later that evening, Lili made some saffron rice and roast chicken, leaving it on the table for her husband to eat if he came home. She washed some tomatoes and sliced them. She put one slice into her mouth; the tangy juice of it bit her mouth. While cooking, she could still feel the afternoon heat on her body. When she reached to take a second slice of the tomato, Shifteh appeared at the kitchen door. A short dark purple dress clung to her slim body.

'Do you like my bird, Mother?'

Lili ignored the question but Shifteh continued, 'My friend gave it to me.'

Lili stared at her stepdaughter.

'My friend is a strong man.' Shifteh took a slice of tomato and tossed it into her mouth, turning at the kitchen door. 'Poor Mother, you don't have friends, do you?' Then she left.

That night went without sleep. Lili took a cold shower. Her husband was late. Back in her bedroom, she stood at the corner of her window, looking outside. In the evening's light and still coming darkness, she heard the neighbour's sheep move; their bells made a pleasant tune in the silence of the night. She felt tired and wished to sleep but anytime she closed her eyes, she heard giggles. Nothing was there. Nobody was there. But behind her closed eyes, she could see the sound as it pressed itself into the body of her bed. She could hear, *Isn't it too hot, Mother?*

She was ten years older than her stepdaughter. Her husband was twice her age. In fact, her own father was only three years older than her husband. At the day of courtship, her husband told her father that he was a widower. But he wasn't. He was a divorcee. His ex-wife ran away with his best friend and left Shifteh at home alone.

*

A few days later, Lili was busy cleaning the house. Her husband was away again. The food she made was still untouched on the table. A fly hovered. She started by vacuuming the kitchen and then she moved to the living room. When she reached her stepdaughter's room, she paused at the threshold, then pushed the vacuum cleaner in. The girl was lying on her bed in her floral-patterned bikini, ice cubes all over her stomach and breasts. The bird was sitting on the bedside table. The birdy feathery odour was in the air. Shifteh stared at her stepmother, her eyes full of poison. Lili vacuumed closer to her stepdaughter. When she reached the corner of Shifteh's bed, Shifteh stretched her long leg off the corner of her bed and, with the tip of her toe, lifted slightly the hem of her stepmother's skirt.

'Feed me, Mother. I am hungry.'

The stepmother pushed herself away from the girl. 'I cook but you don't eat.'

Lili tried to ignore Shifteh, but her stepdaughter didn't want that. Shifteh started to walk around Lili. Sometimes, she stopped the cord of the vacuum cleaner with her feet and sometimes she just danced around her stepmother, touching Lili's hair. 'Oh, what is it, dear Mother? You are lonely, you feel lonely,' and continued dancing and moving her body around her stepmother.

Lili pushed the vacuum cleaner into the living room again.

Once, in the evening, when the light outside was gradually moving into the skirts of thick clouds, Lili had gone to the barn to get pots for the new tomatoes. She walked into the clean air of the barn. The barn smelled of clay. She walked in the dark air towards the shelves where she knew the jars were lined up on the shelves: cucumber pickles, tomato pastes, pomegranate syrups. It was as if all the vegetables were inside their tomb, a mausoleum of vegetables.

Lili stepped into the dusty light in the corner of the barn. Further from the door, Lili felt the darkness press in against her, so that it was choking her. She took another step. She was almost within reach of the jars, when she saw a body. Then bodies. She saw that it was her stepdaughter's legs tangled into a body, wild or human. She wanted to rush outside, but she was stopped by a long arm, big hand. A man's hand. Then she heard Shifteh's voice, coming to her from the tunnel of her fear. She watched as her stepdaughter disentangled herself from the naked man on the ground. Shifteh stood naked before Lili, smiling. Then she reached down for the bird and placed it on her stepmother's head. Shifteh's breasts momentarily pressed against Lili's lips, her closed lids. The smell of sex everywhere. Her stepdaughter put the bird on her stepmother's head, and then while she was buttoning her dress, she whispered into her stepmother's ear, 'I hope you understand you shouldn't say anything to my father.'

Lili felt the sharpness of the bird's toes and she nodded. The man dressed and got on his red dust-covered motorbike and left. Shifteh stared at Lili and blew a kiss in the air to the bird. Then Shifteh reached for the bird and pressed down the heaviness of the bird's flesh on Lili's head. Lili froze, terrified the sharp claws would tear her scalp and eyes. Shifteh grinned, took the bird and left the barn.

*

'This is it,' he tells her, taking her suitcase, pushing her out of the train.

When they reach the house, his eight-year-old daughter sits on the steps at the entrance door. He takes his new bride's luggage inside. The child follows, staring at the woman who comes with her father. 'This is your new Mama.'

Lili sat on the sofa. The girl stood at the doorstep and stared at her. Lili looked around. The weatherboard house smelt damp and dark. The old sofa was dirty yellow velvet. The wooden coffee table was covered with a biscuit tin, some bowl rice and packets of sweets. She could see fingerprints smeared all over the old cracked polish of the wood of the table.

'I will take your stuff upstairs and turn on the hot water. You need a shower,' her husband said.

A week later, he took his new wife shopping. In the train, he sat next to her. She wanted him to go away, far from her. When they stopped, she found the station was big and crowded. He walked fast; she walked slowly. In a matter of a few minutes, she was surrounded by total strangers, some pushing each other, some coming from other directions, some talking to each other, to her, to her, to her. She felt dizzy and nauseous and in the middle of people, he found her.

'I told you stay with me. Don't keep a distance from me. You will get lost.'

Tears covered her face. She hated to be with him and she was frightened by all these strangers. She followed him quietly into the vegetable market.

That night, Lili waited for her husband to return, knitting a baby jumper with white cotton. While knitting, she fell asleep, waking the next morning to find her husband gone again. Lili walked to the kitchen to find Shifteh sitting on a wooden chair, rocking. Two legs of the chair were in the air. She controlled the movement with her big toes.

'Make me breakfast, Mother.'

Lili ignored the girl's order and asked, 'Where is your father?'

'At work,' the girl said, moving her body towards the breakfast table, folding her arm and planting her head on it. Her dark long hair swam on the table.

'I didn't see him last night. I thought he came home. He never tells me when he will come home or when he goes again,' Lili said while looking outside; the tomato plants were standing in the farm shoulder to shoulder on supporting sticks.

'He is a man. He shouldn't tell you anything,' the girl said. Her big black eyes were fixed on the food.

The stepmother ignored the girl and went to her bedroom. Through the sound of her own sobbing, she heard the key turn. Her stepdaughter had locked her in the room.

'Open the door, open it. You silly little girl, open it.'

Lili pushed and pulled the doorknob, but Shifteh was holding the door from outside. And when she felt that the stepmother was pushing hard, the girl let the door open. Lili fell down and her face hit the floor. When she finally stood up, her stepdaughter was standing there, staring at her. The stepmother raised her arm above the head of the girl.

'If you hit me, I will call the police. Police like motherless children. Police support them. Protect them from fake mothers.'

The night after her stepdaughter locked her in, Lili lay down on her bed, a rare night when her husband was in bed too. He slept closer to the door, she near the window. The bedroom window framed the starry sky; some clouds on the move and the full moon watching them. She stared at the sky through the half-closed lace curtain. The fabric was softly moving in the air. She was sleepy but couldn't get to sleep. She got out of bed and wrapped herself in her white bed sheet. The freshly washed fabric leaked into her body. Lili went outside and sat on the steps. The satin moonlight covered the house and the farm. Under the moonlight, she watched a spider weave a white web on a tree from one branch to the other, against the sky. The clouds moved around the moon, her face wrapped by the white fabric of the clouds. The face of the moon appeared and disappeared a few times, and finally the clouds ate half of the moon's face.

From that day on, Lili used to go to Shifteh's room whenever her stepdaughter wasn't home. Lili would lie down on her bed, covering herself with the bed sheet, while inhaling the girl's smell, staring at the ceiling, thinking if only she could return to the time when she first saw her, when Shifteh was just a little girl, a poor little girl with a runaway mother. Of course she would take care of her, she had told her husband the day she walked into this house. If only the girl was a bit younger, you know. Children listen to you when they are younger, much younger.

She wished her husband had come to ask for her hand much earlier, when the girl was just a little one, a baby. Lili liked babies; when they don't know much but are nice – cute and fluffy. Like a little bulb of cotton. That's how they look when they are inside you. Lili had seen a photo of it. They are just a little curled-up white thing in the photo. She had once touched a newborn. She still remembered the touch. She was just a little girl herself, when Lili's auntie gave birth to a bundle of cotton. Lili didn't see how it came out. She just remembered the touch. The cotton bundle was asleep when she walked to her auntie's room. The room was quiet. She could see the baby's breathing – her stomach coming up, going down, under her pink bed sheet. The bundle of cotton was wrapped into her white swaddling clothes. Her eyes were closed and her red face was as soft as the new cotton. Lili wanted to have that baby.

If only she could make her stepdaughter so little she could take her inside her, so that gradually her stomach would grow bigger and bigger until the doctor would say, 'Congratulations, you have a girl.'

*

At night, when Shifteh was out with her strong man, under the reeds of her thoughts and dreams Lili found a touch; the touch of her stepdaughter's bed sheet; her fingerprints everywhere; tomato paste, pomegranate. Lili wrapped her body into the fabric; she inhaled the girl's sleepy body which lived inside the pores of the bed sheet. Then there was a light flashing inside the room through the open window. Lili went to check. It was Shifteh alighting from a motorbike. Lili ran back to her room, went to bed and pulled the bed sheet over her head.

In the morning, the house was empty. Lili sat on her doorstep. The laundry door was open. It was a bright day; white sunlight pollinated the laundry. She stared at two corroded washing machines; an umbrella web above them. She went upstairs to Shifteh's room. At the door, she stopped and scanned the room. She was searching for the bird. The bird was sitting on the bedside table, half asleep. It seemed to Lili that the bird didn't notice her presence, or the bird was just ignoring her entrance. Lili stepped over her stepdaughter's clothes that covered the wooden floor. Lili reached the bed and stripped the bed of its flat sheet. She slowly crept up to the bird, dropping the bed sheet over the bird, then wrapping it around the bird's body. Lili could feel the stiffness of the bird's muscles. She gently squizzed the bird's neck, pressed it harder and harder. She could smell the feathery body which was wiggling inside the bed sheet. Then, she brought the bird to the open window and let go of the corners of the bed sheet. The bird scratched the corner of the window with her sharp claws and flapped. Her wings were clipped. The bird dropped to the ground.

Lili walked out past the laundry, past the boundary of the back fence and into the farm. For a while, she looked up at the blue sky and imagined the shadows of birds flying in the sky. She walked deeper into the field of tomatoes. Then she stopped, pulling first one tomato from its stake, then another and another, so the soil was pocked. She lay down in the soil, smelling its moist face. And planted her belly in the earth.

Swimming

I pushed the wheelchair along the narrow passage between pool and sitting area. I watched children in the pool mimicking the instructor, who was standing on the edge of the pool, bending, and the children were heads down, both arms stretched in front of their faces. Mothers sitting along the wall were changing their children's clothes: wet swimmers, rubber bathing caps, bags scattered on the floor.

'I'll change myself,' Mr Bird said.

I left his bag with him at the entrance to the men's change room and went to the women's change room. I could hear misty voices, shouting, speaking, women and children, sending signals over foggy air. Every now and then, a drop of water fell from the ceiling. I passed a group of young girls in bikinis gathered under one shower head, giggling and talking about a party. I walked past them looking for an empty shower cubicle to get changed. Under the other two shower heads, I saw two naked women, both covered in shampoo foam. I stood outside the shower rooms, watching. Faces and bodies disappearing and reappearing under the steam of the hot water and the smell of lavender shampoo.

*

I remember my first day with the Birds. I was going to have my own job, a paid job. I had already spent all my savings on a car; I'd needed a car. It was one of the criteria for getting my job.

I followed my Tom Tom to find my way around in the Castle Hills area. All the way, I listened to the ABC news read by John Logan. His voice made the most horrifying news of the world sound like free verse poetry. I was in love with his voice. Anytime I pictured myself with a man, it was with a man who had a voice like his.

I checked my face in the car's rear-view mirror and walked through a long brick-paved driveway. At the left side of the driveway, in the middle of a big lawn, there was a gardener, a young man who raised his head and looked at me, or so I thought. I stopped to pretend to answer a call but instead I reversed the camera on my phone to check if my make-up hadn't sweated off. Although I was only a few steps away from my car, I was already worried about how I looked. As I walked past the lattice of poplar trees, a long red-brick building appeared in the distance.

At the door, I wiped my shoes on the WELCOME mat and walked into a dark hallway. A cleaner opened the door at the same time; we acknowledged each other with a smile. I kept the door open for her; she pushed two buckets of water and a mop outside. I stood in the hallway; the light from outside came through two long glass doors. I glanced at myself in the glass, touched the corner of my light red headscarf near my neck. I was so nervous that I hadn't realised Mrs Bird was standing before me. Mrs Bird was tall and slim, wearing a yellow top and pants. With her big white hair, she looked as if she were a tall daffodil.

Mrs Bird introduced herself then led me into her office and then gave me a bundle of insurance papers and a black pen with golden writing: Commonwealth Bank. I sat on a chair next to her and signed.

'Ma..na...dan. How do you say your name?'

'Mandana.'

She tried a few times and then she said, 'OK, Mandy, did you meet my son, Mr Bird?'

'Yes, briefly.'

Then she stared at me and said, 'All is done, please wait outside.'

*

After a while, the cleaner came up the hall again. 'Mrs Bird said you can start tomorrow.'

'Thank you. I am Mandana.' I stretched my hand towards her.

'I am Shossanah.'

We pressed hands, while looking at each other.

'Nice to meet you' came at the same time. We both smiled again.

'There are a lot of windows to clean.'

We both looked at the ceiling to floor windows.

'Yes, a lot. Mrs Bird wants all the windows to be cleaned every week.'

When I walked through the entrance gate, I heard Mrs Bird's voice again.

'Sue.'

*

As I came out of the women's change room, I saw Mr Bird, sitting in his wheelchair, ready to go to the spa. When I reached him, he looked at me top to toe but didn't say a word. I was sure he never had seen a woman in a burkini.

It was the first time I had worn the swimming suit. In fact, it was the only swimming suit I have ever worn. If my mother saw me like this, she would go on saying prayers all day and night, asking God to forgive me for this sin. I had to do my job, and here I was. I don't care so much. It's not that bad. I wouldn't if I had the choice, but work is work.

I moved his wheelchair a bit closer to the spa, where he could reach the metal handle while he leant on my shoulder to stand up and get into the pool.

A woman in a dark yellow bikini was taking a shower in front of the spas. Two of three spas were taken: in the middle one there was a big man wearing a golden crucifix around his neck, and in the spa next to him was a man who was lifting water weights. His eyes were fixed on the woman who was taking a shower in front of the spa.

*

'Where are you from? Are you Lebanese?'

'No.' My feet felt dead. I had never been into a strange man's bedroom before. I stepped back, just one step. Maybe I made a mistake to take this job.

'Come closer. Are you the new nurse?'

'Yes, Mr Bird, I am your new nurse.' I could feel the sweaty fabric

73

of my headscarf rubbing against my chin. Quickly, I brushed the sweat into my headscarf, worrying that it might mess up my face.

He moved his wheelchair and pulled out a map, spreading it on the small table in front of him. 'Show me where you are from.'

I stepped forward; standing close to him, an odour of some unknown medicine silted into my nose. But still I couldn't look at his face. I looked around the blue, yellow and green veins of the world and put my finger on some location around the Caspian Sea,

'Here, from here, and here too.' I took one step back and I stared at him.

*

'She is a qualified nurse.'

'I saw the CV. Are you sure she is strong enough? You should remember my son is a heavy man. I can't help her to move him. She will need to wash him, clean him, and drive him around to places like the swimming pool – that needs good muscle strength.'

'I assure you, she can handle him. I have seen her in the nursing home. She was a basketball player. She has done some kickboxing and martial arts too.'

'In Kabul?'

'No. When she was in Iran.'

'I didn't know women were allowed to play basketball and kickboxing in those countries.'

*

Mr Bird sat comfortably in the middle spa. I sat to his side. The smell of chlorine burned my eyes and nose. I was worried that if my eyes continued to burn I would lose my ability to see or move. How would I help Mr Bird then? My skin started itching under the swimming suit. When my eyes adjusted, I noticed that the crucifix man was staring at me. My legs felt hot each time the bubbles from under my feet rose up and chlorine steamed into my nose.

Nearby, a group of elderly women were waiting for their class. Many of them must have been my mother's age – plump with cellulite thighs and puffy stomach. They looked cheerful. I thought of what my mother used to say: 'A woman's look says everything about her. When you have your first child, you should stop wearing red.' She used to say it to her sisters. My mother had so many self-imposed restrictions. No make-up, no bright colours for women, no long and loud laughter. My mother would never allow herself to be exposed so publically like these women did. But I didn't care what my mother thought of me any more. I liked my job, even with the burkini. The elastic fabric glued my belly and when I pulled at it, the fabric made the small sound of a gulp.

*

Before I moved in with the Birds, I lived with the family of one of my mother's cousin, the Razi family in Bankstown suburb.

I had my own room and bathroom with the Razi, but I had to spend many hours with them. It was considered rude if I ignored them or didn't eat with them and didn't spend some time watching TV with them. They watched *Wheel of Fortune*, *Neighbours* and *Home and Away*, shows which bored and bewildered me. They changed the channel whenever they thought people were about to kiss or make love. One had to pretend to be sexless in this family.

*

Two women, aerobics instructors, exchanged a few words with the crucifix man. He blinked at them and then stared at me again. I ignored him. Music started; it was some kind of techno dance music. Another aerobic exercise instructor appeared at the edge of the pool, joined the first one and started star jumping. The elderly women in the pool mimicked the instructors. Mr Bird sat in the steamy spa, his head rested back on the edge of the spa, closed eyes. The noise inside the pool didn't bother him.

*

Anytime I walked to the backyard for a bit of fresh air, I saw Shoshana busy cleaning the windows, the never ending windows. Each time, we acknowledged each other with a quick wordless head shake because we both knew that Mrs Bird was watching. I liked to sit on a stone bench next to the pond. I used to stare at those windows, everywhere in this house. I like the silence of the day in the backyard, and then, as if frogs sensed that I was there, they were singing from every corner of the garden. Goldfish jumped up and down in the pond.

*

I changed and sat in the café area. I could smell chlorine on my face. The swimming pool was quiet now. The schoolkids' session was over; the elderly people's aquatic exercise was over too. The swimming pool was left with only one young girl still floating about and one of the pool staff in yellow green shirt gathering the ropes, picking up kickboards. The elderly had showered and changed and were gathered outside the swimming pool entrance with the community bus driver.

After a longish wait, I walked over and knocked on the toilet door. 'Mr Bird?'

'Come in.'

I walked into the disability room. He was covered with his towel. I helped with his clothes and put a linen hat on his head. I pushed the wheelchair. The crucifix man was standing outside the spa talking on his mobile phone. The bus driver was trying to start the engine; it spluttered. The driver got out and looked around. The crucifix man went to help the driver. The old people were sitting in the bus and staring at the two men through the bus windows. The bus driver went inside the bus and pressed the accelerator; the oily sound of the accelerator flushed the air. I wheeled past the bus.

*

My room in the Birds' house was a garage converted into a bedroom with brown carpet, a single bed and small wardrobe, a computer desk and two filing cabinets. I spent most of the time in the main house where Mr Bird's room was but I came to my room three times a day to pray. The first time I wanted to pray I had used my mobile phone app and found *Gibla*, then *Kaaba*. North-west meant I had to face the main house to pray. I opened my prayer mat and washed my hands and face before praying. I started in the silence of the evening.

In the middle of my prayers, I saw the door open and the rim of the wheelchair appear. At first I tried to ignore it, but soon Mr Bird had wheeled himself right in front of my prayer mat. I stopped.

'Mr Bird? Do you need anything?'

'What are you doing?'

'I am praying.'

'Oh, sorry.' He sat in front of me.

I stopped. 'You can't sit in front of me and watch me.'

'Oh, no?'

'No.' A stranger is not allowed to look at the face of a woman who is praying. 'You can sit there, behind me if you must. I prefer to be alone when I pray.'

But Mr Bird wheeled himself behind me and waited until I was finished.

'Do you need anything?'

'Yes, I need you to talk to my mother.'

*

After helping Mr Bird to get ready to go to bed, I went back to my garage room and read the Koran. Sometimes, on rainy nights, I sat at the window and watched the reflection of rain from the streetlight running down the crocodile-skin terracotta roof of the neighbour's house. Sometimes, to keep myself busy, I played basketball with a small ball and small basket at the corner of my bed.

In the mornings, I helped Mr Bird to sit outside and have his coffee; the air filled with the sound of frogs, croaking from their hiding corners. I saw his mother was watching us behind the windows.

*

The day after the swimming pool, Mrs Bird called me to her room. 'A help nurse is coming. You have to prepare a bath because his exercise

77

will be in the water.' Then she said, 'Why didn't you wash him yesterday after the pool? He still smells of chlorine. It's bad for his skin.'

The helping nurse was a middle-aged woman, short, with a heavy body; her blonde hair was poking out from beneath her white cap. She spoke to me with a very slow tone, as if weighing each word, as if spelling them to me. 'Don't push, just hold here.'

We immersed Mr Bird's body into the spa bath. I watched her moving the sponge all over Mr Bird's body, over the tapestry of wounds made by the surgeon's knife after the car crash. After washing, we took him back to his bed and covered his body with lotions and powders. Mrs Bird was watching us while drinking her coffee. Then the nurse moved me aside and took the towel off his lower body, powdered his legs and then brusquely moved his penis from one side to the other as if shooing a kitten off a sofa so she could powder the unpowdered area. Mr Bird just stared at the ceiling as if holding the gaze of a pair of hidden eyes.

*

One day Mrs Bird said, 'Ah, Mandy, I need you to do something today. The cleaner called and said she couldn't come. I want you to clean the house, first the windows. I have bowling today and I'm already late. The cleaning stuff is in the laundry cupboard.

I felt a hot stone on my chest. 'Excuse me?'

She repeated herself, but this time slower.

'I heard you Mrs Bird, but no, I am not going to do the cleaning.'

Through an ocean of wrinkles, she stared at me.

'I am a professional nurse. I am here to help Mr Bird with his medication and to drive him around for his exercise and to doctor's appointments. That's it.'

She looked at herself in the mirror. 'I thought when you are not busy, and I have noticed that my son doesn't need your constant attention, and I have noticed that you are spending time reading – I thought instead of reading, when you are not busy with my son, you will clean the house. Besides it is not every day, only those days when the cleaner can't come.'

'No, sorry, I won't do it. I am a nurse and not a cleaner.'

'What is wrong with being a cleaner?'

'Nothing. It is just that I am not one, that's all.'

She left and slammed the door.

I opened the door and shouted at her. 'And Mrs Bird, my name is Mandana, not Mandy. Mandana, mandana means eternal, everlasting, do you understand?' I slammed the door.

*

It rained ten days in May, non-stop. One night, the rain was so heavy that I had to pull over at the side of the highway. I sat in the car and turned on the radio, dialling through bad receptions from waltz music to community radio to unknown languages. I turned the engine off, slid my body down further into my seat and sat there. Then I heard my mother starting to talk on some frequency of dream, with her usual complaints about me not being helpful at home, about me being out all the time, at the sports field. 'I can tell, you think your nose touches the sky.' My mother who cleaned and washed, cleaned and washed, till my father got fed up with it and left. 'Can you stop?' I remember that short sentence again. 'Can you stop?' But she didn't stop and I left home. I don't ring her. Not even to hear about my potential suitor. The rain eased. I turned the engine on and the wipers went right and left sweeping leaves off the windscreen. Through a cleaned arc on the windscreen, I saw a passer-by who had covered his head with a wet sack, running. He was the only one on the road, no one else, no cars. He was young. I wondered about offering him a lift.

Unstitched

Hami crept into the corner of the principal's office and saw his mother there in a chair opposite the principal, with Behrooz, his one-year-old brother, on her lap. Behrooz was trying to escape from his mother's arms and she was struggling to hold him.

The office was small and crowded. Some chairs were squeezed in front of the filing cabinets, where the parents of the boys from the Golden Wattle swim team were already seated, and their boys stood next to them.

Hami saw that Dr Rabbi Zadeh was there too. He was on the other side of the room, near the window, seated next to Hami's mother. They were both watching the school principal, who was writing something down. Benjamin, Dr Rabbi Zadeh's nephew, stood next to his uncle. Benjamin didn't even look at Hami, but rather kept his eyes down on the principal's moving hand, while John, Marcus and Justin, three of the members of the Golden Wattle swim team, did look at Hami as he walked in. In fact, they stared at him, then Marcus made a face, and John and Justin sniggered and looked down.

The school principal's office was humid. The ceiling fan was spinning and the reflection of its three wings was dancing on the whitewashed wall of the office. Hami went and stood next to Benjamin. Both boys smelled of chlorine.

The principal said, 'I have decided that as punishment all of you won't be participating in the swimming carnival this year. You boys have been banned from competing to teach you a lesson that the swimming pool area is not for fighting. Aggressive behaviour will not be tolerated in my school.' The principal started writing again.

Hami didn't really care. Although he was a fast swimmer, he hated the smell of chlorine anyway, but he knew Benjamin would be disappointed. His swimming was as excellent as his study records at school and he'd been keen to join the swim team.

That morning, before their first training session with the team, Hami and Benjamin had stripped off to get into their swimmers. Three of the older boys, John, Marcus and Justin, were already changed and waiting on the benches. Marcus had looked at Benjamin and Hami, scanning down their naked bodies until he arrived at their genitals, his gaze lingering on the circumcised tips of their penises. Marcus nudged John and Justin, pointing and whispering. Then, as if as one, the three boys from the Golden Wattle team stood on the benches and started chanting, 'Broken dicks, broken dicks.' Hami had no memory of throwing a punch, but he remembered the expression in Marcus's eyes when the blood began to flow from his nose.

Hami and Benjamin and the three boys were sent home for the rest of the day. The Golden Wattle team members and their parents had exited the main entrance of the school and had remained huddled together for a while, whispering and gesturing, before shaking hands and disappearing into shiny dark European cars and four-wheel drives.

Dr Rabbi Zadeh and Benjamin followed Hami and his mother and little brother out the side gate of the school to a café at the end of the street. Hami sat close to his mother as she exchanged a few words with Dr Rabbi Zadeh. Sometimes when his mother spoke in Farsi he could drift off and almost pretend not to understand. Hami drew closer to his mother when he noticed his father approaching. Even before he saw the face, he knew the man, the only man in the street wearing a tailored light grey suit and a light blue silk tie. When his father reached them, Hami watched as his father moved his gaze between his wife and the doctor, lingering on the two of them, the outstretched hand of Dr Rabbi Zadeh ignored and left dangling in the air. Benjamin's uncle left his hand extended and finally Hami's father shook it.

'Sorry I am a bit late. The barber shop was busy.' Hami's father spoke too loudly, with too much drama.

Hami watched his father run his fingers through his newly trimmed hair.

The table was small and Hami's mother was sitting cramped, holding Behrooz in her arms. Behrooz's face was puffy, his eyes were closed and he was wrapped in a light blanket. He'd been circumcised last week. Dr Rabbi Zadeh did the operation. Hami put his finger on the sleeping boy's cheek. It was hot and red, like lightly barbecued marshmallow. He poked the face a few times.

His mother complained. 'Leave him alone. You wake him up. He would want to walk around – you know it would hurt his wounds.'

The boy stared at his father. His father's big light brown eyes were fixed on the street, as though he was entranced by everyday life: cars blowing horns, children screaming, people waiting in the line to use the teller machines, the smell of coffee, of baking, of car oil, the sweet feeling of business; the life of migrants and refugees; the smell of homesickness wrapped in the air.

'So how was the school meeting?' His father asked.

'They are banned from swimming carnival,' said the doctor.

The waiter came to take their order and Hami's father raced to order first, then both Dr Rabbi Zadeh and his father started the customary complimentary competition about who would order and pay for the tea and sweet. And the school meeting was forgotten.

The waiter soon returned. As he placed their tea and sweets on the table, he said some words that Hami was used to only hearing at home. '*Noosh-e-jan.*'

Hami's father put a tea in front of Dr Rabbi Zadeh and one for his wife. He also put the rosewater Turkish delight on their plates. After putting his own tea and sweet in front of himself, there were two extra sweets left in the tray.

His father put one in front of the Benjamin and one in front of Hami. 'Although I ought to give you boys nothing because you were banned from swimming competition, I will forgive you both because I had a very good customer today.'

Hami touched the white-dusted Turkish delight with his finger, the sweet pillow. The white sugar dust printed on his finger. He looked at his mother with a smile. His mother's sweet smile was her language. She dipped the crystal sugar stick into her tea; the sugar cracked and cried. She stirred it, sipped the tea.

Dr Rabbi Zadeh and Benjamin left when their tea was finished, leaving Hami's family sitting for a while because his mother hadn't yet finished her tea.

'So still this local hospital doesn't have a Muslim doctor?' the father asked his wife.

'No.' His mother paused, taking a sip of tea. 'Dr Rabbi Zadeh is a good doctor.'

'Yes, but still it annoys me that my boys should be circumcised by a Jewish doctor.'

'That's the reason I trust him,' his mother said and smiled at Hami, who was still playing with white sugar dust.

'I mean, as a doctor. Who is better than a Jewish doctor if there is no a Muslim doctor in the hospital? ' Hami's mother looked at Hami and with her long fingers spread a kindness into her son's untamed hair.

'Operation?' His father said with a mocking voice and sarcastic short laughter. He pulled Behrooz towards himself, held him up briefly, examining the still sleepy boy until Behrooz began to squirm and cry, then he passed him over to his wife again.

'You are talking as if he performed brain surgery. In our country, every old woman who delivers a baby does the circumcision. It is just a little cut. They used to do it with a scissors. They didn't need surgical equipment. You should know that better than I do. You lived your whole life in the village before I married you.' He drank his water down in one go, then he flicked his finger on his tea glass; the little sounds of ding ding rose in the air. 'The doctor is a good customer, though. He always chooses very good quality fabrics.' He looked at his wife and two sons. 'Good taste.'

Hami was bored. He let his feet dangle, swinging backwards and forwards. Almost as though he meant to, Hami's left leg swung too far and kicked his father's shins. His father flinched and leaned in close to Hami. He felt the heat on his father's face.

'Be careful, boy,' his father shouted.

His mother quickly moved her son towards herself. Hami tried not to look at his father's face.

*

Hami lay down on the red velvet sofa in his tailoring shop to rest. The three wings of the ceiling fan were spinning over his head. As he stared at the ceiling, the quiet sound of electricity filled his ears. It annoyed him.

He sat up again and stared at the big radiology envelope on the coffee table in front of him. He stared at the label on the envelope, with his mother's name, her date of birth, and the date and the time the X-ray was taken. For a while, he played with the corner of the envelope and then took the pictures out of the envelope. He held them up to let the light pass through the picture. It was his mother's breast in the negative picture. This was the latest X-ray; the one taken of her right breast. X-rays from her left breast were all piled up in black cabinet in the corner of his tailoring room, this room, his room now. After the mastectomy of her left breast, he thought everything was finished. That was just before his father died. Now they'd been free of him and of cancer for almost six years. Behrooz was away studying chemical engineering at a university in Queensland, and it was just Hami and his mother at home. Then her right breast started to discharge a dull fluid that both of them knew.

'I will show it to Dr Rabbi Zadeh to see what he thinks. Mum trusts him very much.' Hami let the X-ray slide from his fingers and lay back on the lounge. For a while, his eyes were fixed on the ceiling and then he lowered his gaze to his belly where his hands were resting. 'I might see Benjamin too.'

Hami had barely seen Benjamin since high school had finished, not since Benjamin had gone on to study medicine. Hami had always

84

known he wouldn't get into medicine at university, not with all the hours working with his father after school, but he'd hoped to study something, perhaps even stay in contact with Benjamin, but his father forbade him. Regardless, Hami had secretly tried enrolling into university. He tried for nursing.

'You have healing fingers,' his mother had told him once as he had helped his mother to clean his one-year-old brother's wounds. 'Poor little thing,' his mother had said, watching Hami's hand cleaning Behrooz's wounds of circumcision. 'You have healing hands,' his mother had said again when he had carefully dressed her wound after her first surgery.

When his father found out that he wanted to be a nurse, Hami had heard as his father screamed at his mother. 'What? I will kill him myself. I would rather die than see my son doing a woman's job. Nursing? Nursing is for women.'

So Benjamin went to university to become a doctor and Hami learnt how to cut suit patterns and then to do the stitching.

*

Hami was twenty-two years old when his father died. He was alone with his father in his room when his father breathed his last breath. He watched his father's eyes. Hami didn't let his mother come in. It was the first time he had refused his mother anything. Hami looked into his father's light brown eyes, which still were open, and he could see his father's dreams were moving inside them. Hami knew those dreams. They were replicated inside his own eyes, as if dreams were suits tailored for life. As his father's oldest son, he had to carry on the family business.

The first Friday after his father's death, his mother didn't prepare for guests because they didn't have any close family members in this country. But Doctor Rabbi Zadeh came with Benjamin and Benjamin's mother. From the tailoring shop, Hami could hear his mother and Behrooz's voices as they greeted the unexpected guests at the front door and then walked them past the shop, where Hami was tailoring a new suit for a new client with a big business importing grapes. Hami didn't pause his work and was surprised when there was a knock at the door. He knew it was Benjamin because he knocked the same way when he used to come to pick him up so they could walk to school together. There was a short rap followed by a softer second tap.

Benjamin let himself in. The friends shook hands and hugged one another.

'Come and sit.' Hami pushed aside the half-finished jacket laid out on the red velvet sofa to give Benjamin some place to sit, and then he went back and sat on the chair behind the sewing machine, spinning it around so that he faced Benjamin.

They looked at each other and smiled.

'It is strange thing to see you here, sitting where your father used to sit, doing as your father used to do.'

Hami stood up and took a plate of halva his mother had made and offered it to his friend. Benjamin refused it with a small shake of his hand. Hami put down the plate and sat down, next to his friend, on the red velvet sofa.

'It is weird to see you here.'

'No, my friend. What is weird is that I am now running this business.' Hami searched for Benjamin's attention, but Benjamin was looking down at his hands folded across his belly.

Without looking up, Benjamin said, 'But your father prepared you for it right from the start.'

'That's right. Since I was almost eight years old.' Now Hami's eyes were looking down too.

Both friends were quiet for a while.

Then Benjamin broke it. 'Guess who I met last week?'

'Who?'

'Marcus.'

'What? No. Where?'

'At the gym.' Suddenly Benjamin wanted to have a piece of halva. The plate was on the table next to Hami. Benjamin stretched his arm over to reach the plate himself, stretching his body towards the table, leaning on Hami's thigh to keep his balance. He pressed his elbow down harder onto Hami's leg but still couldn't reach the plate.

Hami took the plate and offered it to him. 'My mum made them. Trust me, they are very delicious.'

Benjamin broke off a piece and, while looking at Hami, put the sweet slice in his mouth. Hami took a piece too. Benjamin fancied another one. This time, each of them took one big piece and ate it. Benjamin looked at Hami and Hami smiled.

That was eight years ago and the last time that Hami had seen either Benjamin or his uncle.

Now his mother's new cancer was coming to invade her body again. Hami got ready and fixed his hair in front of the mirror. 'You have your mother's face,' his father had said a few times when Hami was standing before him wearing the suits of other people, on the few occasions when his father's gaze would lift from the suits to Hami himself. Hami brushed his hair with hand. His mother had trusted Benjamin's uncle. Perhaps he could trust Benjamin too. Hami decided to go see him in the hospital.

*

One afternoon after school had finished for the day, Hami was helping his father in the shop, when his mother walked in. She was holding a bolt of silk fabric under her arm and she asked if Hami's father would make a dress with it for one of their neighbours. It was autumn. Hami was doing stitches on one of his father's customers' jacket. Sitting at the corner of the window he could see the neighbour's backyard. The neighbour was sweeping up some leaves. In the last few days, strong winds had blown dried leaves into their backyard. His father asked Hami to clean it. In her stooping posture, the neighbour carried her broom around the backyard and piled up the yellow-brown dried leaves into a corner. It was difficult to imagine her in the silk dress on her granddaughter's wedding.

'That old woman wants to wear silk,' his father said, testing the texture of the silk. 'You know I don't do women's dresses. Take it back to her.'

Hami shuddered, lost control of his work and his thimble fell down, rolling along the wooden floor and landing next to his father's feet. Hami leapt from his seat to pick it back up. As he reached for it, his father stepped on his hand, his soft leather loafers cutting across Hami's fingers so he yelped. His father took no notice. He tasted the silk, first with his fingers, then with his lips, before pushing the fabric aside. He returned to the suit on his cutting table and with one hand on the table and scissors in the other poised for a moment mid-air, he began to cutout the pattern. The boy could feel the thickness of the fabric from the sound of the cutting. *Kerrikh, kerrikh*, the sound of the cutting in the air.

*

Hami no longer had any tolerance for blood, or cutting, or sewing a stitch. The level of his mother's pain was beyond his strength. He washed the wound. The stitches looked strange, supernatural, as if from somewhere else. It didn't belong to this body. The stitches were rough to touch and the location of her lost breast looked like chalk lines on fabric. The lines criss-crossed her body as though they were hiding something; as if they were hiding her breast under her skin. After gently washing his mother with a sponge and bowl of scented water, he helped her to get dressed. Alone, back in his room, he only was capable of one thing: crying quietly into his pillow.

Five times a day, he helped his mother to prepare herself for praying. He prepared the ritual dust in front of her because she couldn't do the ritual wash. He helped her to sit on her prayer mat and instead of standing up with each *sura*, she prayed seated, only bowing.

After her first operation, she couldn't wear clothes that touched her stitches, so Hami went to the market and bought soft cotton fabrics. At night, when his father and mother slept, Hami went into the shop and made comfortable dresses in bright colours that he knew his mother would like and that his father wouldn't frown upon too much. Those nights he would try on his mother's dresses pulling the soft fabric on his body to test the softness, to make sure it wouldn't hurt his mother's body. He looked at himself in the mirror, wearing the dress he made for his mother to make sure the dress looked good and his mother would like to wear it. He imagined his mother in this dress.

'It is so comfortable, and the fabric is so good, where did you find it?' his mother asked when she tried it on.

He looked at his mother on the mirror. 'Don't tell Dad. I made it myself.'

Now his father was dead, he made all of her dresses, with soft fabric in reds and pinks, some with floral patterns. Sometimes, when his mother felt a bit better after her second operation and when the chemotherapy wasn't making her too sick and she had enough energy to go out, Hami would take his mother to the front yard to sit under the sun and have her tea, or to the fabric shops, where the shopkeepers knew him as an excellent tailor. They had known him since he was a little boy, coming to the shops with his father. Hami watched closely as the shopkeepers unrolled bale after bale of different fabrics for his mother's inspection. With her broken English, she would haggle for a lower price and with the same broken English the shopkeepers resisted giving in. He would watch them, thinking to himself, 'If I stitched those two broken English together, I would have one long nice unbroken sentence.'

Now he made his mother's dresses openly, she, not he, would try on the designs with their pins and paper, inside out and seams showing. She looked at her son in the mirror while he used the scissors to fix the sleeves or collar, and gave him advice. She even became his manikin for men's clothes, changing behind the curtain and coming out in men's suits, then standing on the stool in the centre of the room so Hami could do the adjustments.

One day, after she was recovering from her right mastectomy, she'd said, 'Turn off the fan, Hami. They hurt my stitches.' Her face looked pale, run out of blood.

Hami was stricken that he'd asked too much of his mother, but she reassured him.

'That bloody little breeze from ceiling was penetrating into my body.'

He looked at her little fragile body. Then he looked at his own image in the mirror. Over the years, he had watched himself grow inside other men's clothes. As if he had lent them his body. Now that he was the one who was running the tailoring business, he asked his mother to try those half-made suits on. He had watched his mother pose in men's clothes when he fixed suits for businessmen. He had watched the four corners of the tall mirror rusting with time, as though time itself had gotten old in the corner of his father's tailor shop. The same shop which was his and would make him get old too. He sent his mother away and lay down on the red sofa and fell asleep

*

The tailoring room looked clean. Hami tidied up the cutting table and put the scissors and cutting papers in their boxes. The piles of half-cut clothes went into the cabinet. He made a new file for his mother's medical reports.

Hami was wearing a new black suit, with a black silk tie, one that he'd splurged on the fabric for, a blend of cashmere and cotton. There was a bouquet of flowers with black ribbon on the table.

Benjamin walked in with a black jacket in his hand. 'Wow, look at you,' he said and sat down on the corner of the velvet sofa. He looked at his friend in the mirror.

Hami was fixing his tie.

'Where did you get that suit? Don't tell me you made it yourself.'

'This material cost me a fortune, my dear friend.'

'Good taste. I have to come to you for my next suit.'

'Do you want to try it on?' Hami slipped out of his jacket and handed it to Benjamin, taking his friend's jacket from his outstretched hand.

Briefly, the two friends admired each other's image in the mirror. Then they exchanged again, each wearing his own jacket and ready to go out.

Hami noticed that the tag was still hanging from back of Benjamin's jacket. He cut it, laying the tag and the scissors down on the table, and then followed Benjamin out of the house, where Hami's mother was waiting. She was walking slowly around the front yard, her hands on her back. 'She looks better today, even in a black dress,' Hami thought. He had made her dress too, spending far too much on the velvet and silk.

Hami turned to his friend, almost whispering, 'My mother was very fond of him. Your uncle. Peace be upon him. She always trusted him.'

Satan Hill

I was a horse when the puck possessed Akram.

The puck came to possess me but couldn't, as a horse's belly and heart point towards the ground.

I had two black shoes on my hands and two black shoes on my feet as my hooves. I was that brown-bodied, white-maned horse on the other side of the river that used to come down to the river to drink. I was dancing on my hooves to the sound of drums when Akram appeared on the hill.

It was dark when Akram finally appeared at the edge of the hill where the whole family gathered to have dinner. It was sunset and the light of the dim bulbs was made dimmer by the flies that swarmed over them. Dogs were tired of chasing cats; cats were tired of chasing hens and roosters. Hens and roosters were locked up and dogs and cats were sleeping side by side. Mothers cooked, girls washed, and men swatted the children that swarmed as thickly as flies.

She stood at the corner of the veranda, charcoal-black eyes burning like two condensed fires, but I was the only one to see those fiery eyes, because she wouldn't let any human close to her. Her jaws shook, her hands shook and she shivered despite the heat that everybody could feel by looking at her eyes.

'Don't stand there gaping at me, come and help set the dinner!' Akram's mother called out. When her mother came close enough to see her eyes, she noticed under the firelight that her daughter looked strange. 'My god, what is the matter with you, what is it? Have you been bitten by a snake or something? Look at your eyes. What is it the matter with you?'

'She has been possessed by the puck,' said the old man sitting on his veranda smoking his pipe. 'We have to catch her, put her inside a dark bag, hang it from the tallest poplar tree and swing it until the impure spirit comes out of her. If you delay doing that, the puck will mix with her spirit and possess the whole of her and nobody will be ever able to separate them again.'

The old man's eyes looked quite puckish if you asked me. From where I was watching him, as I played on my hooves I could see his red eyes through the orange and yellow flame of fire on which he was making his food.

'I knew she would get possessed. I saw her while I was coming down from Satan Hill checking on my tea fields. I saw her lying on her back, her chest and heart towards the sky,' said the old man with puckish fiery red eyes.

'Why didn't you stop her?' cried her mother.

'Who can stop a young girl with a mind as strong as the rays of the sun and wild as summer wind? Your daughter doesn't listen even to God. And I am warning you, the puck loves strong spirits with a wild mind,' said the old man.

'Don't stand there looking at me like frozen cattle, do as he says and save my girl,' shouted the mother at the watching men.

A few of them moved towards her, though nobody dared to touch her.

Akram had lain on the warm, humid grass beside river, not far from the rice fields where she worked. She could smell the fresh seeds they planted each day. After work, on her way back home, she passed many squares of paddy fields, in the middle of a vast green plateau, and big piles of uncultivated green seeds waiting to be rooted in the clay. In some fields, she could see women still working on their land, bending over with big piles of seeds in their hands and babies sleeping on their backs that looked like humps. She could hear some of them singing. In this season, every farm worker had to work hard, as the shortage of rain before cultivation dried out their reservoir and they had to sow as soon as they could before the paddy field water evaporated.

After passing Satan Hill, she decided to rest for a while, so she lay down and closed her eyes. She was soon in her own world, and with eyes closed could hear the quiet water of the river and the big bell of her cow that was shuffling around her. At rest, she felt the numbness in her fingers recovering and leaving an itching feeling that pleased her. She breathed deeply, feeling the fresh air in her lungs. She felt itchy, a ticklish itch in her body, especially at the left corner of her heart just close to her nipple. She felt its itchiness increase. She breathed deeply again, then she felt hotness at the edge of her heart. She fell into a deep sleep.

When the sun was going down behind the misty rice fields, where the sun became less concentrated and looked like village girls' cheeks after climbing Satan Hill, orange-yellowish, she woke up. First she opened one eye, where at the edge of her eyelashes she could see the sun's rays reflecting in many different directions, then she realised it was almost sunset and she had to go back to her village.

Now a woman brought a black, big sack. Men gathered around to catch her. After a tussle, being bitten by her strong teeth, and scratched by her nails, they took her and put her inside the bag and closed it. They carried it to the tallest poplar tree and hung it there. Then they swung it many times until the movement became circular. The centrifugal force would take the puck out of the girl's spirit.

It was full moon and I was on my hoofs dancing around the tree. I could feel the heat of the bag coming out of the circles. They did this until the grey cloud came and covered the moon and the village became pitch-dark. Then they left the girl and went on with their business.

In the early morning, they took the bag down from the tree and opened it. She was sitting there with fiery red eyes.

'She is still possessed,' said the old man.

'We have to swing her again,' said a woman from the crowd.

'There is no use. A puck has possessed her with the same gender as her. The spirit of the puck is persistent when the puck is from the same gender. It makes it impossible to separate them, because the two spirits feel so comfortable and in harmony that they become one as soon as the puck possesses the body,' said the old man.

'What should we do now?' asked a man.

'We have to keep her isolated, send her to the other side of the river, otherwise she will possess our children,' said the old man.

They sent Akram to the other side of the river and there she stayed. No one saw her or talked about her after that incident except for her family who, every year at cultivation time, remembered her as a very hard-working farmer and missed her work.

I missed her too, but I forgot about her very quickly as I was only four years old when the teenage Akram was possessed. Now I am grown up, almost the same age as Akram when they put her in the dark bag and swung her to take the puck's spirit out. I am a hard worker too; working in tea farms at Satan Hill is not an easy job. I work for the old man. After work, on my way back to the village, I rest in the corner of the river. It feels good. I lie down and close my eyes, the river is quiet and calm and I can smell tea from every farm. I feel sleepy. Something is itchy inside me, right at the left corner of my heart, close to my nipple. I feel a soft and pulse-like itch.

I go back to the village before dark; otherwise that old man will give me more to do tomorrow. I look at the other side of the river, at Satan Hill's skirt. There are a few horses walking slowly. I see a small puck, a little one next to them. She is playing with them; she has two black shoes on her hands and two black shoes on her feet, as hooves.

Delirium

The sound of children playing marbles was reverberating in the walls and pouring down the stairs. I was lying down and looking at a tapestry. It had a woman's face with yellow eyes in silk and woollen brown hair. Its cheekbones were pomegranate-red, a mix of silk and cotton.

I had just been injected with morphine and my eyes were getting sleepier, drawing all the pictures from the carpet into my sleep. There was no sound of a nurse's plastic shoes walking on plastic floors. My ears were emptying of all sound. I could only hear the morphine, which was burning inside me. I was at home.

On the day they brought the tapestry, nails were hammered, a pair of hands moved in and out of my sight. The smell of wool, silk – sweaty – after each injection. Gradually, the carpet seemed to collect the sounds and noises of my surroundings, was gathering them into the thick wool, into the patterns and flowers. The flowers under my body became bigger and bigger and the sounds became whispers. I felt lighter.

When I woke up – I don't know if I woke up or I moved into another sleep – I saw that she was there. Her thick wool coat was becoming the face of the snow in the backyard. In my half-awake, half asleep state, she didn't have a clear face, as if half of her body had melted and frozen into the air. I opened and closed my eyes a few times till I could make a form for her face in my head. Her red and white shawl looked like the snowmen's outside in the garden.

Marbles poured down the stairs and their sound shattered my dopiness and my face became submerged in the woollen flowers. They were soft and fresh; I plunged my fingers into the heart of the carpet, where I could feel the knots, made by small fingers like mine.

I opened my eyes again. This time she was standing right in front of me without the slightest motion. Her eyes were hazelnut and her hair brown. We both stared at each other, me with real eyes and she with silk and woollen eyes.

She had a red satin dress on. It looked like the one she had on when she came with my brother. My brother who was only three years older than me, yet between my sleeping and waking he had grown. Like a man. Like my father. As usual, he took a vase from the wardrobe and replaced the old flowers with new ones. He seemed to be filled with our father: his affection, kindness, the tall slender body, the gaze. He sat at the corner of my bed; I stared at the clock ticking slowly on the white wall. He left after exactly one hour. When he left, the hair-raising sound of plastic shoes on the plastic floors of hospital wards started to come close to me and a cold hand and a syringe pulled up my sleeve and gave me a dose. Soon the edges of sound flaked away and I fell asleep.

In my sleep, there was a hand – my father's, or my brother's – which injected me. I used to dream that I was dancing around the house in my wheelchair or I was lying on carpets and smelling them. The red roses smelt like pomegranates and the green curlicues on the edge of the carpet smelt of a little village girl's scarf washed with olive oil soap. We used to play hide and seek.

Then I became sick and after that everything smelt like morphine.

I had to wake up again. Things had changed, I could hear whispers swimming under the carpet; days were changing their skins to nights and nights to seasons and again it was the end of winter, a week before New Year. My mother and my aunties were washing carpets in a big shallow pool and my sister was crying and shouting, 'Take it out, take it out, please. The carpet is drowning.' We watched how the carpets submerged into the pool and how the face of the woman drowned; colour was diffused on the surface as if her heart was bleeding. Her hazelnut eyes were crying when they unchained her from the wall and took the carpet into the water.

She was coming close, close to me. I smelt of morphine and she smelt of perfume and her mouth tasted as if it was a ripe red pomegranate. She took a red satin dress from her suitcase and put it on. My brother was there, but I couldn't see his face, his face was cold. I don't remember if I was awake or dreaming the pain, because I was numb from my injection, but I think I saw my father kissing a woman in a red satin dress. When I woke up, no one was around. The room's silence was squeezing my heart. I and the carpet woman were gazing at each other.

Now, the face had been washed away in the carpet cleaning, but she was always in my dream. I could see her hands caressing me. I didn't know she knew me, because on the first day she came, she asked my brother everyone's name but I refused to introduce myself.

Now, maybe she asked my brother in a whisper, 'What is her name and why is she in a wheelchair?'

But it was impossible. I was sure I didn't know this old wrinkled woman. She looked like one of those old women, in a blue hospital gown, who walked with four-legged frames and, like turtles, peer in each room at night. Was it she or my mother who one day brought a small carpet and left it in my room? The night-shift nurse moved it to the corner of my bed and I opened it. Was I awake or in morphine dreams? I saw them all. All my family packed and left. They went to Australia. They sold everything except this carpet.

That night, the night-shift nurse came close to me again, pulled up my sleeve and, at the point where it was already bruised, gave me another shot. My fingertips felt soft and numb, like those little fingers which knotted the carpet, knots so soft and small that we as kids could put our fingers into it and count the small dots. I stared at those hazelnut eyes and they pulled me in. I was running inside the garden of carpets, flowers and plants created roots all over the floors and the smell of moss covered me. I was running inside the second and third floor rooms.

The room on the third floor. A suitcase beside my bed. On a dressing table, a comb with strands of black hair, a pair of long lace gloves, a lace hat and a red satin dress which still held the shape of a body. A man was sitting on the corner of my bed. His eyes, which were hidden behind his dense grey eyebrows, were staring outside. He was my father or my brother. When she arrived, they offered her my room, since I was in a wheelchair and couldn't go upstairs.

I danced on my wheelchair and reached my brother's room. He was in bed with a woman whose red satin dress was hanging from the metal frame. A white plate full of red pomegranate kernels was sitting on the table, left for after lovemaking. I ate.

Marbles reverberated inside the walls and its storming thunder pushed me down stairs. I didn't know if I was asleep or awake. In front of me, a small carpet was hanging on the wall. The middle pattern was empty and instead of the woman's face there was a hollow. Outside, before New Year, they were washing carpets and my sister was shouting and begging them to take the carpets out before they got drowned. Outside in the pool, under the moonlight, a face was emerging from under water. It was a woman's face with yellow silk eyes and brown woollen hair. Her gaze was fixed at the sky and the moon was touching her face. I took her out of the pool.

The weather was chilly cold, like the day I came here. Inside her room, she was sitting on her wheelchair. Everybody introduced themselves except her. Her brother whispered her name and told me why she was in a wheelchair. They all loved her so much that they made a carpet for her. They hung it on the wall before she woke up from her morphine sleep. I picked a basket of pomegranates and made a plate for her. I made a red satin dress for her brother's wedding day. Most of the time I used to sit next to her, listening to the marbles the kids were playing upstairs. Sometimes, the thundering sound would wake her. She told me about smells she felt were coming from the carpets; whispers grew inside the carpet roots. They gave me her room because she couldn't go upstairs any more.

The old wrinkled woman was walking in the hospital ward again. They were trying to help her to walk again. She was sliding her four-legged frame on the plastic carpet and the sound was moving inside the walls and reaching me. I ran away from her, dancing on my wheelchair. I passed all the corridors and reached my room. my room smelt of moss; carpet roots covered everywhere. There was a suitcase sitting next to my bed. On my dressing table, a comb which had strands of black hair from years ago; a pair of laced gloves, a lace hat and a red satin dress which still held the shape of a slim and small body. There was a woman next to my bed looking at a man who was sitting on the edge of my bed. There was a carpet hanging on the wall. The woman's face on the carpet was old and deformed. Everybody had packed and left, all gone to Australia. They sold everything except this carpet. Outside in the backyard, a man was waiting for me.

Now all the walls were dancing around me, carpet roots were rotting, the colours of their flowers fading from continuous washing, the sound of marbles locked up inside the walls. I looked at the mirror. My face was old. A beauty spot which once was firm and dark like a precious pearl now looked like it was dripping from my face. I hear whispers flowering closer and closer.